Keeper of My Heart

An Illustrated Collection of Love & Romance Poetry
by M. Griswold

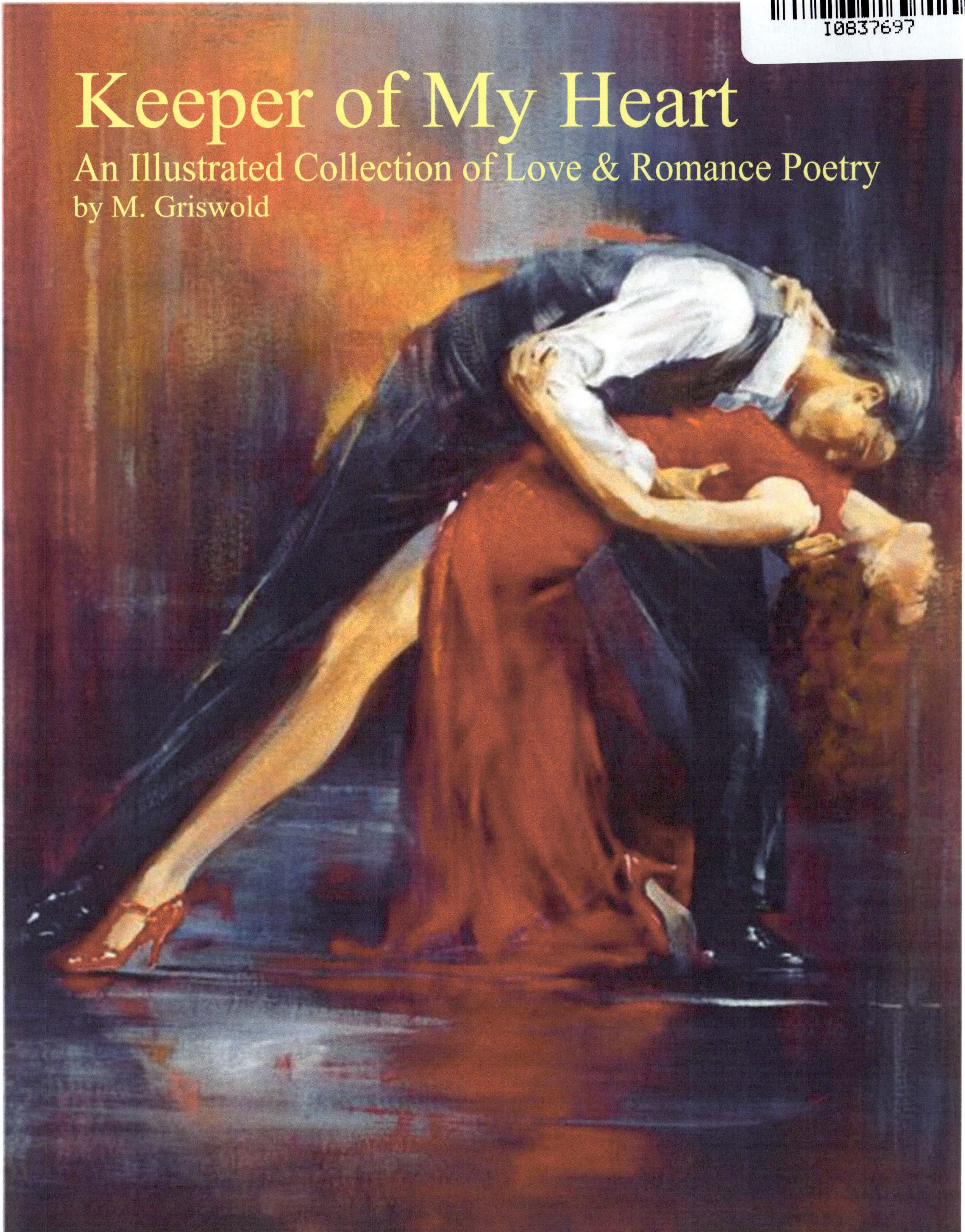

Table of Contents

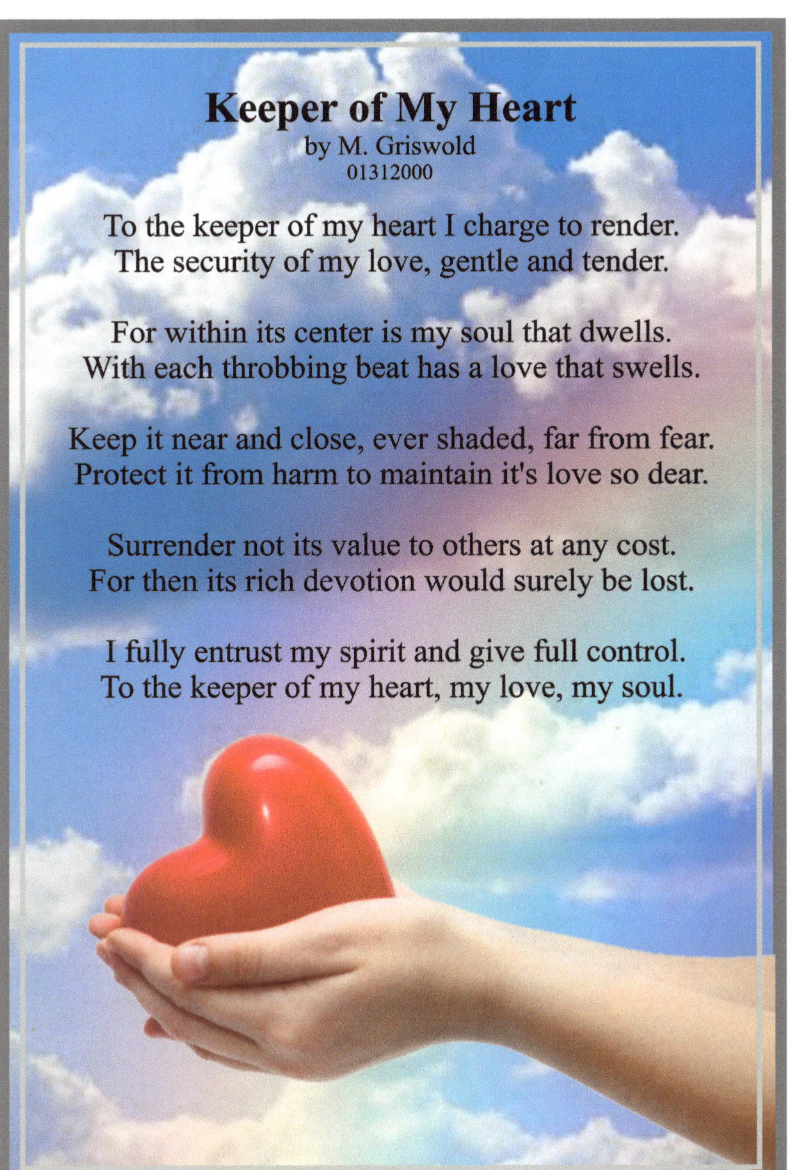

Keeper of My Heart
by M. Griswold
01312000

To the keeper of my heart I charge to render.
The security of my love, gentle and tender.

For within its center is my soul that dwells.
With each throbbing beat has a love that swells.

Keep it near and close, ever shaded, far from fear.
Protect it from harm to maintain it's love so dear.

Surrender not its value to others at any cost.
For then its rich devotion would surely be lost.

I fully entrust my spirit and give full control.
To the keeper of my heart, my love, my soul.

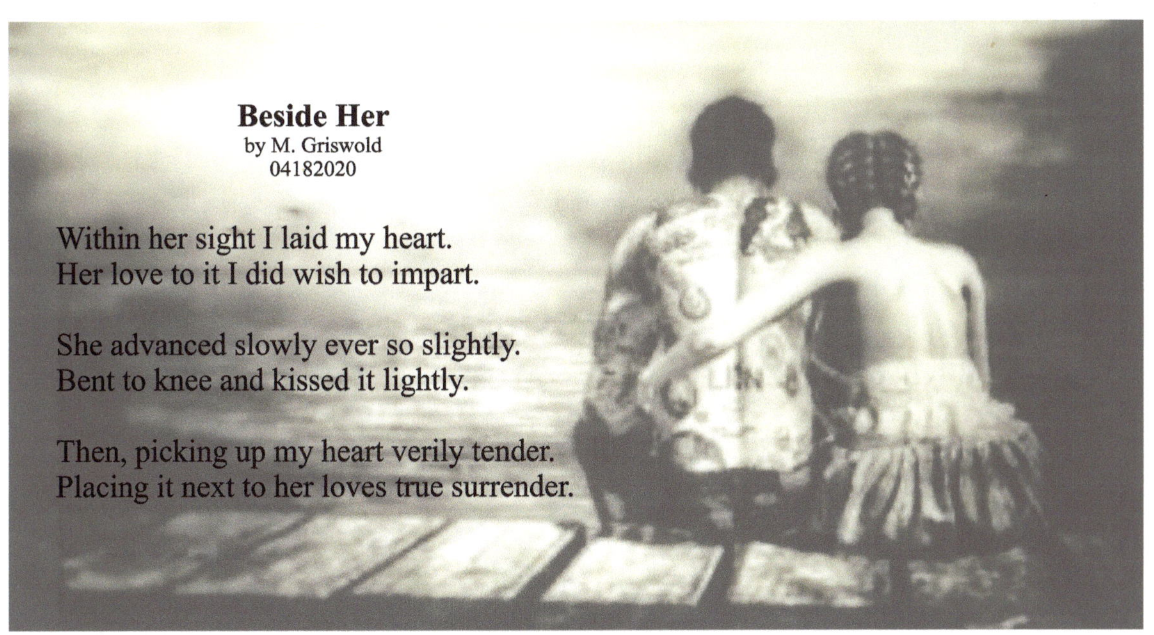

Beside Her
by M. Griswold
04182020

Within her sight I laid my heart.
Her love to it I did wish to impart.

She advanced slowly ever so slightly.
Bent to knee and kissed it lightly.

Then, picking up my heart verily tender.
Placing it next to her loves true surrender.

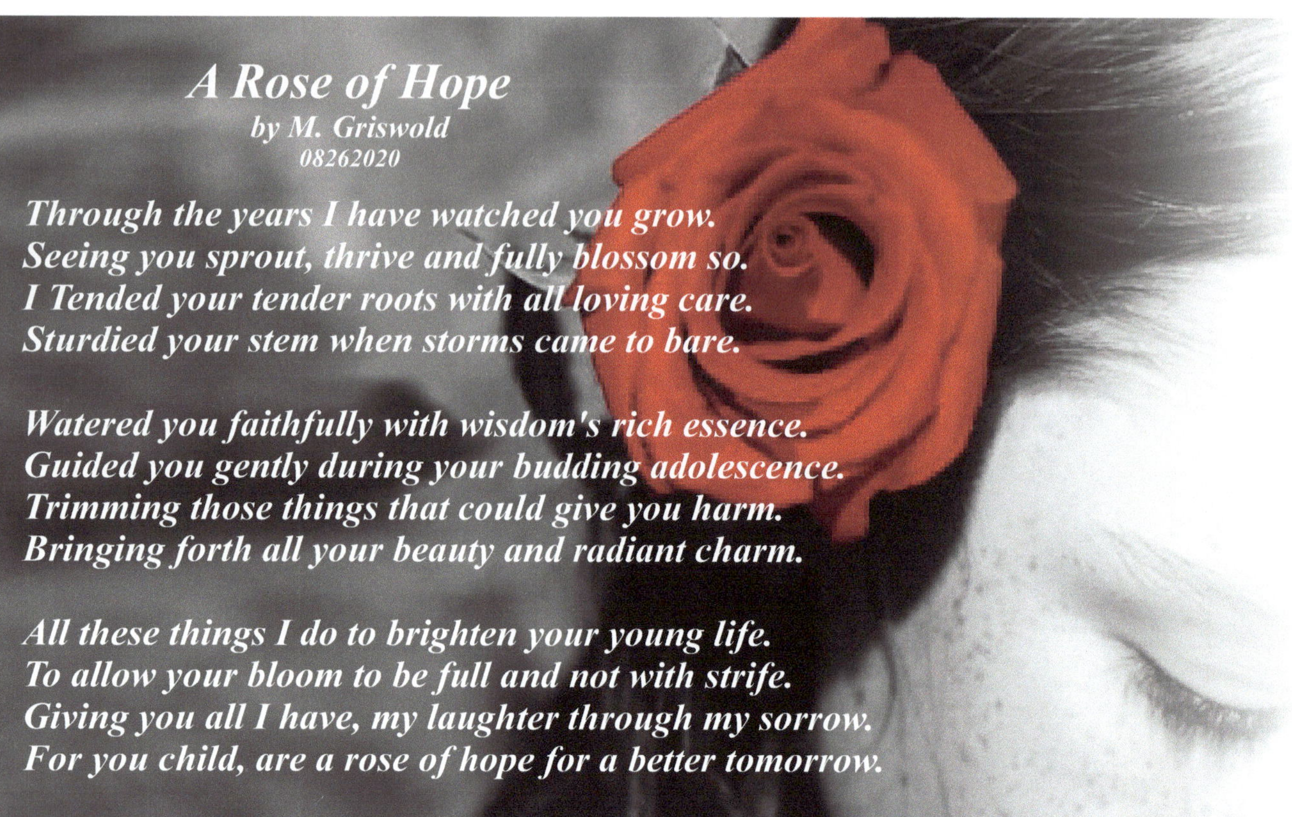

A Rose of Hope
by M. Griswold
08262020

Through the years I have watched you grow.
Seeing you sprout, thrive and fully blossom so.
I Tended your tender roots with all loving care.
Sturdied your stem when storms came to bare.

Watered you faithfully with wisdom's rich essence.
Guided you gently during your budding adolescence.
Trimming those things that could give you harm.
Bringing forth all your beauty and radiant charm.

All these things I do to brighten your young life.
To allow your bloom to be full and not with strife.
Giving you all I have, my laughter through my sorrow.
For you child, are a rose of hope for a better tomorrow.

Footsteps Tread
by M. Griswold
07222020

I walk the park in my loneliness's sorrow path.
Footsteps empty tread one then the other I go.
Meaningless they are echoing crunching the trail.
Shimmering in it's beauty is the fluid quite Quail.

Rounding my path I spy a couple holding hands.
Remembering us, reminding me of my long sad.
Footsteps empty tread on, one after the other I go.
I pass them and smile but inside my heart is crying.

Coming upon the nest where a feathered couple built.
Again thinking back to the spring as we watched in awe.
Now it is empty just as this path I walk terribly alone.
Footsteps hollow tread on, one then the other I go on.

I walk this park, the Quail, today and into the morrow.
Listening to footsteps, remembering within my sorrow.
Footsteps hollow for now tread on, one then the other.
Until that time we walk together upon some distant shore.

A Rose Given

By M. Griswold
05182020

A rose given in the spirit of love's true ember.
For that special someone to always remember.
Of a passionate love that is forever growing.
For a desire of caring, this emblem showing.

It's vivid beauty and romantic scent.
A thorny stem for effect of love's torment.
All these elements do fully symbolize.
Those many facets of love to visualize.

There is no sweeter gift given than this.
Bestowed out of love's yearning richness.
For love's true measure makes life worth living.
And matters most when sharing and giving.

This simple gesture of a flowering bloom given.
Sorrows to be forgiven, powering love onward driven.
So be mindful to always kindle love's golden ember.
By a token of your love, a rose given as to remember.

Across Any Distance
By M. Griswold
010600

Our love does travel across any distance.
Straight to our hearts without any resistance.

No wall is to thick, nor parapet to high.
For this love to overcome, it will never die.

The longing we feel is unyielding in its extreme.
Pulsing with our spirits in a passionate stream.

Currents of desire that flow over a wide expanse.
Ever growing in power by two hearts rushing prance.

On wings of lightning speed direct in their course.
This essence is delivered straight from its source.

Never will it be misguided nor be led astray.
This love will always transfer without any delay.

With love's hopes and dreams sent along the way.
Our future is assured, of this I can truthfully say.

A love so clear, sent straight forward to construe.
Like a sharp arrow it strikes a bulls eye's center true.

Across any distance our love will always transcend.
Over time and eternity, always beginning yet never to end.

Never Again
by M. Griswold
07242020

Now I lay this heart to rest.
I tried to love my very best.
Passions and feelings given true.
Sharing my all in all loving you.

In sorrow, I weep and put away.
Feeling and passions felt today.
Never again this love to make.
Never again this heart to break.

A Rose in the Mist
by M. Griswold
07202020

Within the many shafts of a dawn's prism shine.
A rose in the mist glistens with heavenly design.
Heavily it drips tears of a nights dimming decline.

This rose is over laden with mist's sparkling dew.
Each pedal shimmers within it's own special hue.
Some in purples, others in red's of a brilliance true.

The mist is wisped by the mornings gentle currents.
Caressing each bloom to a quivering disturbance.
Delightfully, they unfold in twinkling transference.

This Rose now warmed from a new morning's ado.
Reflecting love so full, moist with richness anew.
This rose in the mist, I see, is most wonderfully you.

Fool in Love
By M. Griswold
07072020

A fool in love will accept many of things.
With all the joy and turmoil that it brings.
So willing are they to ride out the waves.
Even to the point of digging their own graves.

A fool in love will give most all their things.
Their soul, their spirit and all within that sings.
So willing they are to give up a foolish heart.
Even to someone that will only tear it apart.

A fool in love does things to gain their desires.
It matters not the cold of ice, or the heat of a fire.
They won't pause for those things they require.
So long as they arrive to that which they aspire.

A fool in love lives only for their selfish passion.
They are willing to finish in any form or fashion.
Even when the end is just ragged, unending pain.
The fool in love always stays for love to remain.

Forbidden

by M. Griswold
06092020

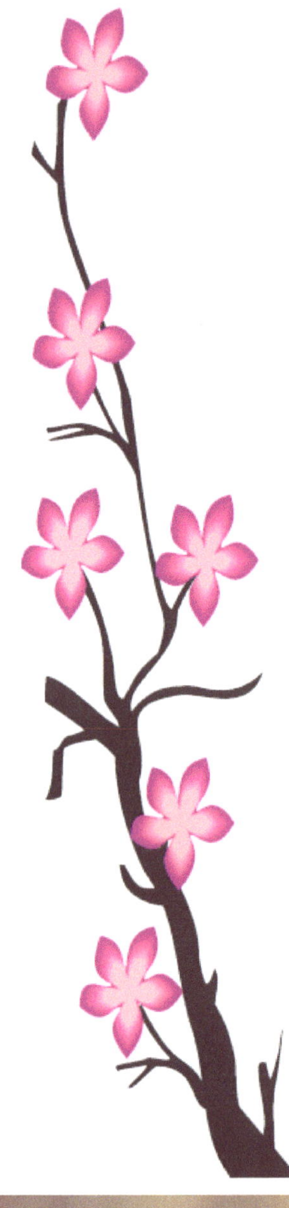

You're a forbidden fruit
that is ripe on the vine.
To pick you, to eat you,
then lick your sweet rind.

Emotions erupt
with jubilance untold
as my lips tenderly caress
your jewel I now hold.

Sweat flows from my pores
like dew in the Spring,
anticipating the taste
of your flavorful sting.

My heart rapidly quickens,
as I plunge to your soul.
Sweet juice on my chin,
my passions out of control.

Faster and faster
I devour your tasty meat.
Completely I'm engulfed
by my raging hearts heat.

Together we mesh
from two into one.
Sensations burst forth
like a new rising sun.

To ravage you so,
with such total desire.
Is sinful I know,
but my soul is on fire.

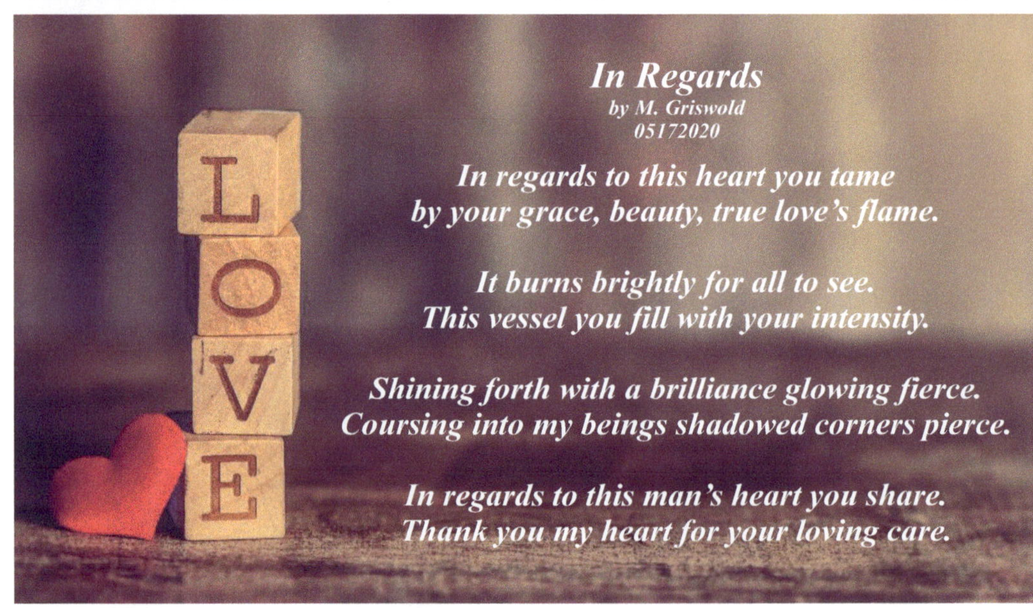

In Regards

by M. Griswold
05172020

In regards to this heart you tame
by your grace, beauty, true love's flame.

It burns brightly for all to see.
This vessel you fill with your intensity.

Shining forth with a brilliance glowing fierce.
Coursing into my beings shadowed corners pierce.

In regards to this man's heart you share.
Thank you my heart for your loving care.

Show and Tell

by M. Griswold
09092020

If you show me yours and I'll show you mine?
And then we'll see if we're two of a kind.
Just show me a little, maybe of your middle.
So we can solve this case of ours, this little riddle.

Oh, I see that you have a belly button right there.
Let me show you mine so we can compare.
See, I told you so, mine's the same as your button.
Cept'n your's is a inny and mine's an outty butt'n.

What else you got that's the same or isn't the same.
Come on reveal it, you don't have to be ashamed.
There ya go I knew you could do it after a while.
I didn't know you and I have the same great smile.

P.S. Bet ya thought I was writing about something else.
    "Smile";0)

Remember

by M. Griswold
12132022

Remember me when you're far and away.
Remember the warmth I left you this day.

Remember the kisses we pressed to our lips.
Remember my gentle smile's loving glimpse.

Remember those times, happy and sad.
Remember the closeness that we have had.

Remember our laughing full bodied in jest.
Remember the stories told in darkened rest.

Remember that gleaming love within my eye.
Remember a shared tear of a cried goodbye.

Remember, most always, my love for you.
A love beyond passion by this heart so true.

Remember these things that are far and away.
Remember my love which grows day by day.

Another Day Without You
By M. Griswold
06222000

Another day without you.
Another day to be alive
within sorrow's empty heart.
How do I survive.

Loneliness surrounds me.
My other half is gone.
Half of this whole is missing
from this souls loving song.

No notes I sing this morning
to greet this new day.
No smiles I bare in caring.
I have lost them along the way.

Another day without you.
Another day's dark dawning.
Another day your love is missing.
Another day in anguish longing.

My Valentine Statement
(hold this in front of a mirror
to discover my secret.)

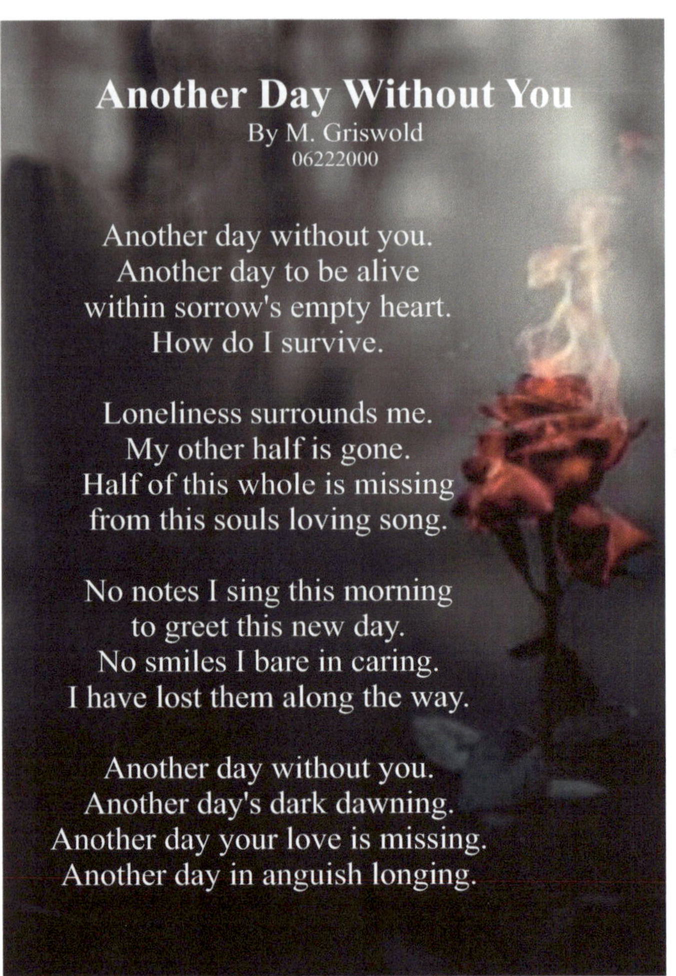

Remembrance's Kiss
Mitchell R. Griswold
07162020

As I peer from my window this cold darkened night.
A slivered pale Moon slowly glides into my sight.

My thoughts slowly drift along it's sloping long form.
I can't help but think of you and my heart that's forlorn.

A lonesome kiss escapes from my trembling lips press.
It's spirit is blown by the wind of a broken heart's quest.

Landing lightly upon a dim Moon's lowly, hanging hook.
My kiss awaits the retrieval of your long yearning look.

Now, as I peer wanting into that darkened, cold night.
Awaiting a sweet kiss returned in kind loving flight.

The night seems darker, colder as I realize gazing there.
My kiss is but a lonely, longing remembrance's stare.

Into Your Heart
by M. Griswold
07272020

Into your heart I've given and anchored my soul.
My love given freely and fully all in it's whole.

You've beaten down the walls that once were there.
By the constant surety of truth that you freely share.

No choice had I of those passions for You that grew.
Within a chest that had only anger and hate for You.

Not knowing the depth of love that You, for me held.
Over time, I found You in me to be so fully in dwelled.

For you see, I had not the choice nor a chance to depart.
Your sacrifice of love completely won my hurting heart.

For all that we've been through and for all we now know.
This emotion is strongly attached and shall continue to grow.

I realized from my beginnings, as I am sure even more now.
You were calling me within my spirit for your truth to endow.

So into your hands I commend myself, oh God, my heart to bare.
For Your way is my way, my truth, and my life forever to share.

More Today Than Yesterday
by M. Griswold
12242022

I love you more today than yesterday, and tomorrow greater still.
For this heart is a cup running over and yet never to fill.

Bubbling within a fever of a passionate sense.
My love grows steadily, past, present, and future tense.

Yesterday I loved you little, today I love you more.
Tomorrow my love will triple by yesterday's today, and tomorrow's sweet amour.

No greater has there ever been a love so fierce of will.
For I love you more today than yesterday, and tomorrow greater still.

Massage

By M. Griswold
09032020

Soft music streaming, the candle's low glow flickers.
Sending you into a daze of convulsing, slow shivers.
Harmony in motion are my hands upon your skin.
As I supple your flesh to the tones soothing rhythm.

I caressingly work in gripping, swirling, soft motions.
Upon your smooth, firm skin I apply a full, rich lotion.
The oil is warm as it is applied so smooth and gentle.
With the touch of a lover's attention to muscles general.

Your muscles become clay under hands of form molders.
Rubbing and kneading, easing knots likened to boulders.
Soothingly pushing then probing, I cultivate your pleasure.
To tenderly relax those tensions into their full measure.

Laboring my way gracefully over your body laying naked.
Creating within you a calmed feeling most bodily sedated.
Sensually stroking those point of your angelic smooth torso.
Then lightly slipping my hand to inner thighs, oh so slow.

As I gently touch, with light grip, some loosened oily flesh.
Your inner thigh meat I kneed like dough, kindly to mesh.
Applying Oil again to places which need more moistening,
I slowly careen down to your feet, who by now are rejoicing.

As if my lips were kissing each and every tender, small toe,
fingers purse and sensually loosen your tense joints as I go.
Each limb taking in its share of the full feeling sensations.
As soreness retreats from attentions tantalizing stimulations.

In finishing you off, I lay with you in total passionate love.
Of the kind that is only spent when love is sent from above.
Then lying there together I whisper sweet words softly to ear.
Gently bathing within our glow by the shadows dancing near.

Gentle Thoughts

by M. Griswold
07202020

So gentle are my thoughts of you.
Feelings of love so tender and true.
Filling this heart to fullness whole.
Ever to render this joy into my sole.

Burning richly in my center's space.
I yearn to envision your smiling face.
Oh, but for a reality of a life that holds.
Our passion, our desires now to unfold.

A wine that has not yet met it's season.
I leave to ripen and grow is my reason.
Yearning still for a matured beginning.
Is my love forever and never thinning.

It's certainty will surely always be there.
Within my sight of that love we share.
Forever and a time we will make it so.
Our love, this feeling shared, to always grow.

Diddle Me Do

by M. Griswold
01062000

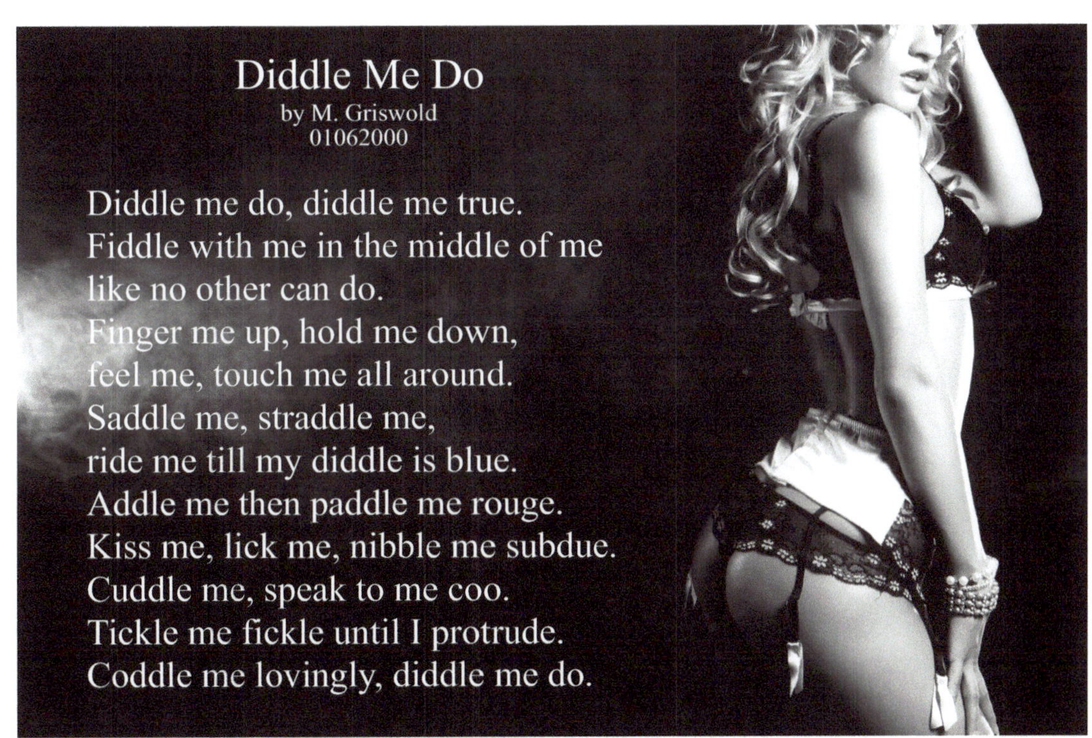

Diddle me do, diddle me true.
Fiddle with me in the middle of me
like no other can do.
Finger me up, hold me down,
feel me, touch me all around.
Saddle me, straddle me,
ride me till my diddle is blue.
Addle me then paddle me rouge.
Kiss me, lick me, nibble me subdue.
Cuddle me, speak to me coo.
Tickle me fickle until I protrude.
Coddle me lovingly, diddle me do.

Captive Heart
by M. Griswold
08282020

Alone now, I do solemnly indwell.
Within this, my hearts, passion cell.
Held for prisoner by isolations hell.
I'm a captive under your loves spell.

Every morning as I alone do awake.
In hopes with you, our love to make.
Then, in my loneliness, I'm overtaken.
Realizing that I am alone and forsaken.

Our love no longer clothes me to adorn.
This, my soul, has now been fully forlorn.
Within my rejection I so longingly morn.
For love that once was in us is now torn.

Why did you, keeper of my heart depart?
What was the crime that was bitterly tart?
Was it of loving you as beautiful living art?
Or was love to much to receive or impart?

I cry as I press this living sadness addressed.
Against these walls I'm wholly am depressed.
I await to be released of this prison of stress.
But captive still, my hearts in love I confess.

Life it seems is this sentence for loving you.
A lone prisoner within spirits wrenching rue.
Is there nothing that I can speak, plea or do.
That will acquit a verdict of my love so true.

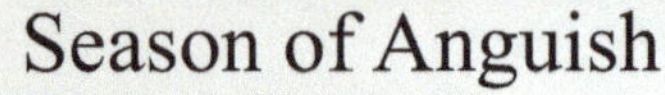

Season of Anguish
by M. Griswold
08272020

From ember to ember in raging force
a heated fire builds to attain its course.
Of passionate flowing is this torrid flame,
erupting from within that which it came.

Never to know the love that it burns for.
This soul is in storm from its molten core.
To touch, but not touch its life's counterpart.
Is a season of anguish for this yearning heart.

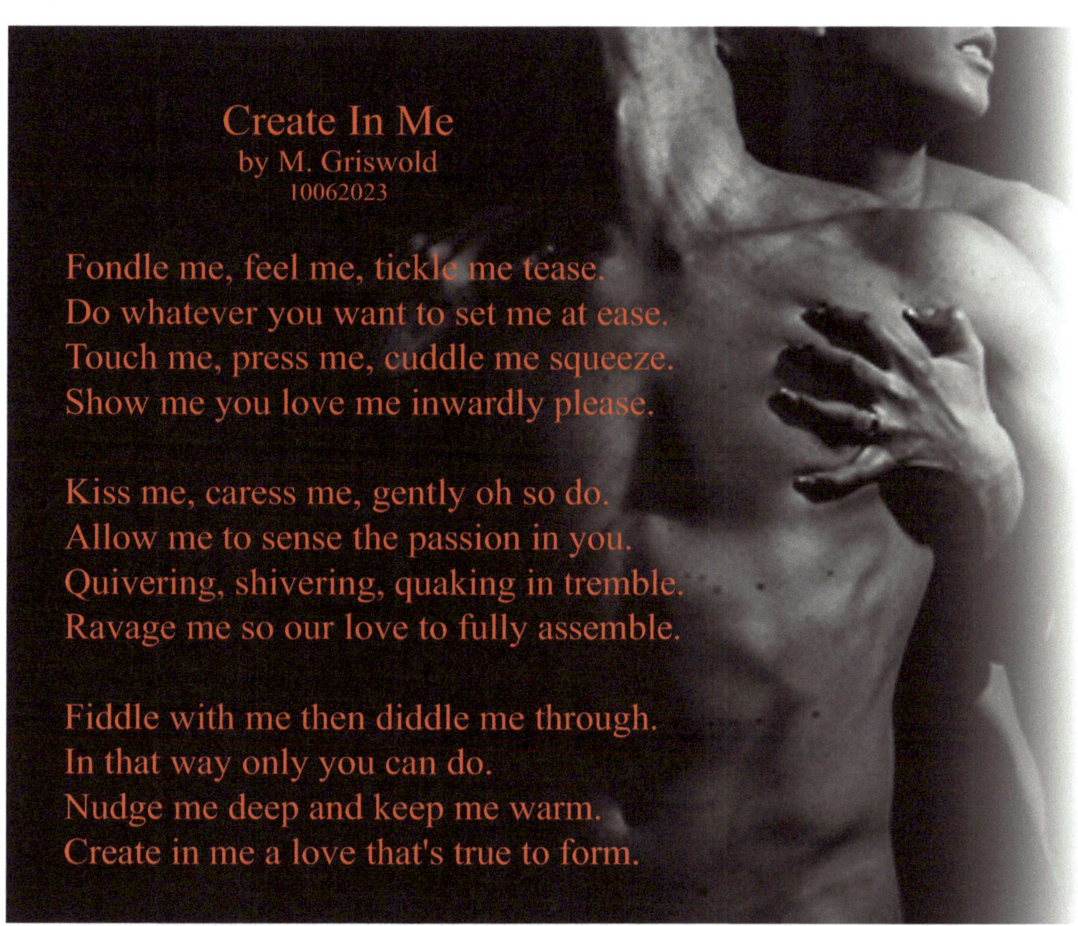

Create In Me
by M. Griswold
10062023

Fondle me, feel me, tickle me tease.
Do whatever you want to set me at ease.
Touch me, press me, cuddle me squeeze.
Show me you love me inwardly please.

Kiss me, caress me, gently oh so do.
Allow me to sense the passion in you.
Quivering, shivering, quaking in tremble.
Ravage me so our love to fully assemble.

Fiddle with me then diddle me through.
In that way only you can do.
Nudge me deep and keep me warm.
Create in me a love that's true to form.

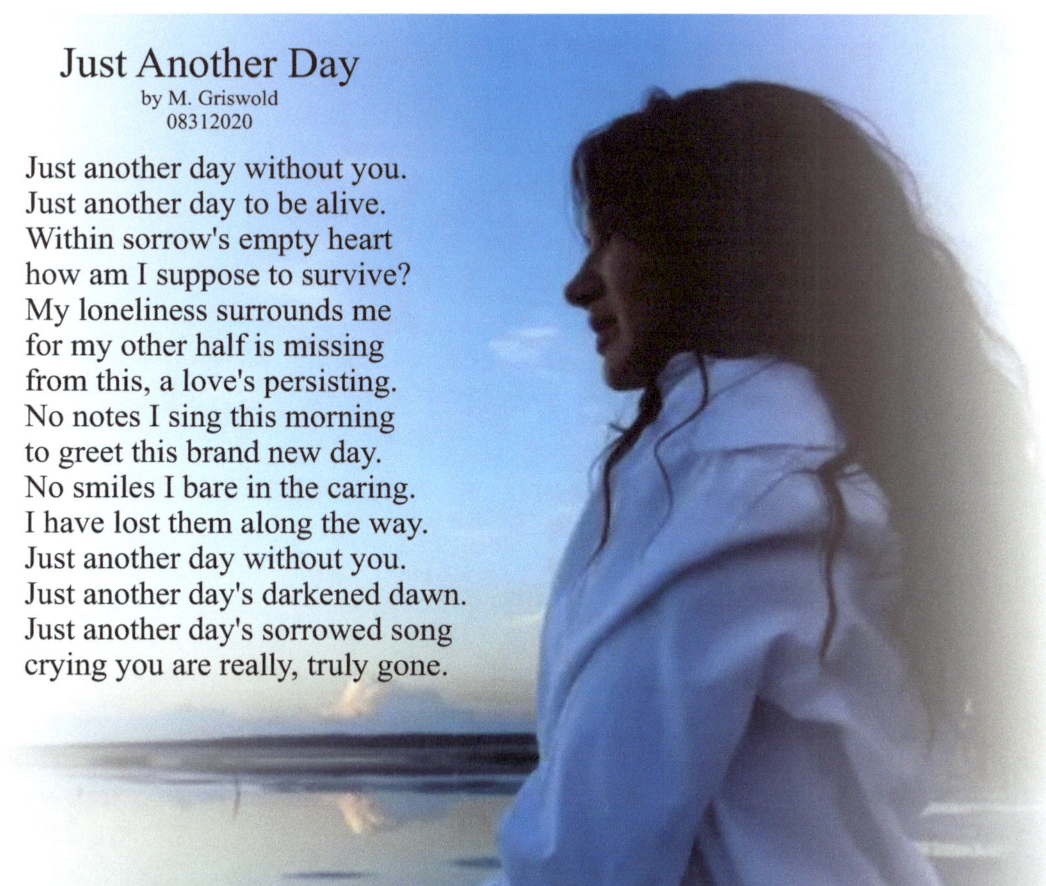

Just Another Day
by M. Griswold
08312020

Just another day without you.
Just another day to be alive.
Within sorrow's empty heart
how am I suppose to survive?
My loneliness surrounds me
for my other half is missing
from this, a love's persisting.
No notes I sing this morning
to greet this brand new day.
No smiles I bare in the caring.
I have lost them along the way.
Just another day without you.
Just another day's darkened dawn.
Just another day's sorrowed song
crying you are really, truly gone.

Love Me As I Love You
By M. Griswold
100200

To have you love me as I love you
is a wish I have so heavy and blue.
To have you care as deep as I do
would create in us a love so true.

To know my love is returned in kind.
To finally be quelled and not confined.
To never seek again your love to find.
To know our hearts are fully entwined.

To have you love me as truly I love you
is this wish for us I have in full passions due.
Happiness and love to fill each day anew
to have your love through and through.

For you're the keeper of my souls heart.
No matter if we're together or far apart.
Because I have loved you from the start
is why I'm writing you this note to impart.

My Sweet Poison
by M. Griswold
05032020

A cancer, a poison you are to me.
I was warned but just didn't see.
Because of the love I hold for thee.
I am now committed to your toxicity.

Why won't you change for love of us.
Why be consumed by your selfishness.
Why must you live within your mistrust.
Why are you crushing my heart into dust.

I know I am not perfect and make mistakes.
I know that I am difficult for goodness sakes.
I do care and love you fully with all my heart.
But the poison inside you is tearing us apart.

Yet, I know that you just don't really care.
About our lost love that I alone must bare.

For My Love's Sake

By M. Griswold
07152020

Feelings and emotions are two of life's delicate things.
If left in the open, unguarded, hurt is all that it brings.
Shown to someone that you think is very special and true.
Only to have them torn up and then thrown back to you.

My emotions I share only because I wish to love and dare.
To show how much I'm willing to share how much I care.
My passions are no game nor toy that can be easily bought.
But it seems my feelings to you, are worthless as not.

I have shared them with you and still you carelessly persist
in playing within a game that you can't humanly resist.
Caring not about any of my feelings nor any deep desires
you selfishly think of self and what you want to transpire.

You hide behind words like "It's only for fun, just a little jest."
Then continue on with my heart as a play thing to fully test.
There is no jealousy on my part, no, not even one little bit.
Just a few of love's passions and feelings that I must forfeit.

But alas, it seems that I am forever more that silly love's fool.
Because I cannot hide my inner feelings for you or from you.
Sharing them again and again for all of my heart's love sake
with the hopes and fears that them you won't continually brake.

I know now of the selfish games you play and which is a foot.
Yet, still I press on for the respect from you, to fully take root.
I will not be taken by surprise again with a self-centered ego.
When all my emotions are returned, twisted and jumbled up so.

I was willing to put up with anything just to be your lover and friend.
For I have foolishly given my heart again to it's own tragic bitter end.
Now, I choose to hide from you what is left within this heart of mine.
Because you are not deserving of my love, not anymore, not anytime.

by M. Griswold
09212022

You're essence is sensual, your body divine.
With a flavor that's sexual, most finely refined.
To eat of your moist flow, I'm most inclined.
With a frenzy of a lover, I begin my sweet dine.

Chocolate melted, rich, creamy and flowing.
Confection thick, passions now ever growing.
Your drops desirable, tempting, ever showing.
In layers rich flowing, growing, never slowing.

Coming to rest upon my tongue out stretched.
Of a wondrous taste exploding, crazed, etched.
My soul is ablaze with your thick flow fetched.
Running down my chin, a dribble not catched.

A delightful feeling erupts from deep within.
I delve in closer from my elbows to my chin.
Your scent is most insane beckoning therein.
Suckling you so frantically, I eat you all in.

Oh, my smooth chocolate, my sweet candy desire.
Streaming, steaming, it's your richness I require.
No other will do, no other can completely inspire.
The love and lust I have for you sets me full fire.

Nearer
by M. Griswold
03292020

Nearer our love two hearts a quiver.
Quiver for love's passions true shiver.
Shiver together so love will deliver.
Deliver to us our essence nearer.

It Would be Nice
by M. Griswold
07162022

It would be nice to make a wee bit of love.
But only if you wish, I don't mean to shove.

It would be nice and oh so naughty of you,
if you'd warm to the idea of a li'l bitty screw.

It really doesn't matter, I'm not so horny you see.
But it would be nice if you were hornier than me.

Love's Scarlet Passions
by M. Griswold
08112020

Blood red is the nights passions flow.
A shade of scarlet in pastels to show.
Hotter than molten, we are swept away.
For tempest passions we show this day.

Bright fevered love we engulf to discover.
Tasting all flavors of life newly recovered.
Spirits merge through currents raging flood.
Of human emotions in steamy thick blood.

Scarlet passions shared for a few moments.
To last all our seasons in total enjoyments.
No guilt is felt for this nuptial filled torrent.
Of our love decreed by God's own warrant.

Now, I know the scarlet passions seems so right.
For love has merged from two to one this night.
So rich is our jubilance within our love that be.
These scarlet passions flowing from you to me.

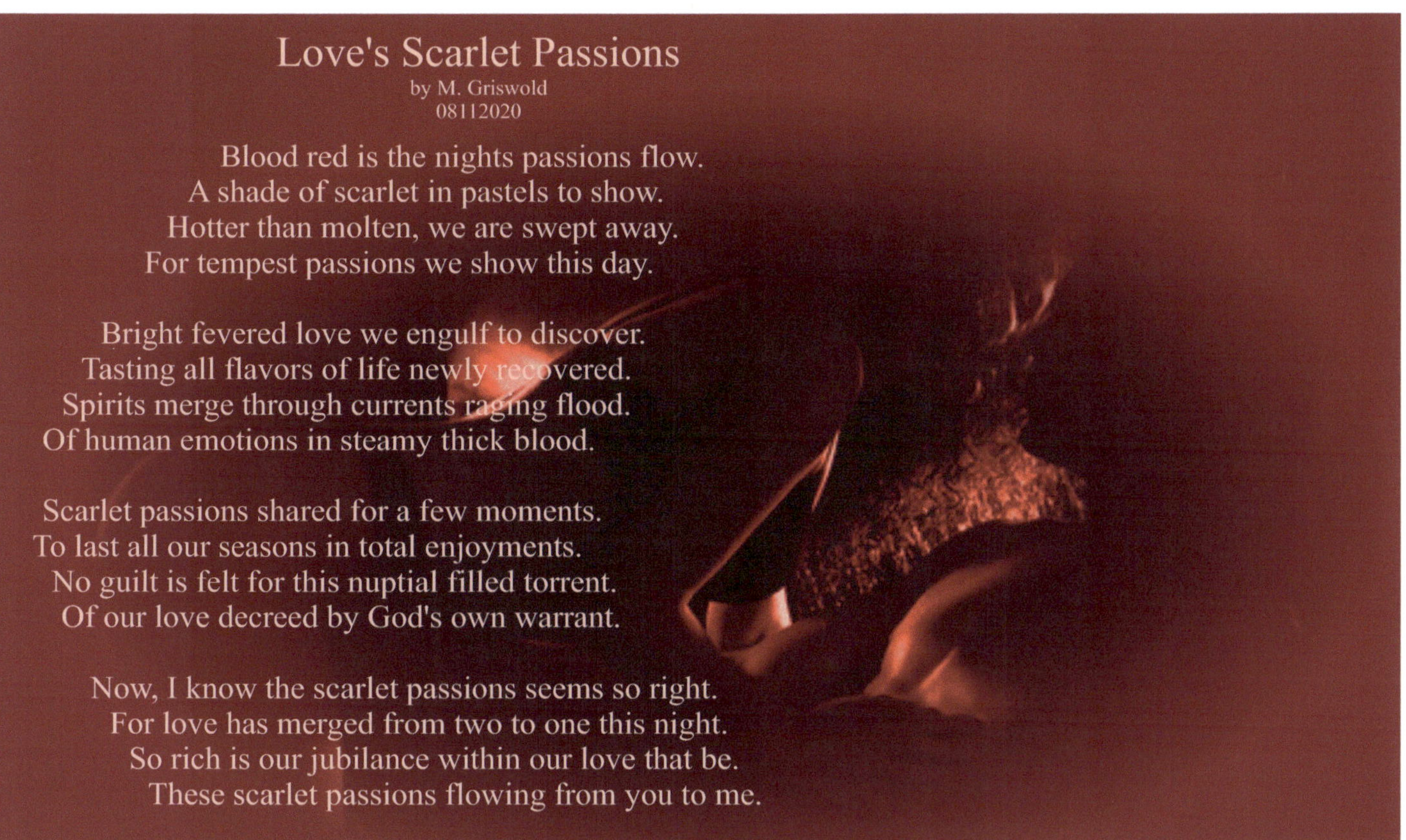

Whisper Me Deeply
by M. Griswold
08032022

Whisper me a melody of a passion dance.
To make my heart race in a lover's prance.
Play for me in a soft caressing harmony.
Those gentle verbs of a soothing symphony.

Whisper me into a slumbering, easy rest.
Of a quiet form till my heart is undressed.
Love me into that dreamy filled state.
Where we lay evermore, our love to create.

Whisper me arise into the morns new dawn.
In loving words warm of a passion's song.
Feed to me breakfast of your selfless being.
Kiss me firmly to insure our souls full sealing.

Whisper close to my ear that you care for me.
Whisper me deeply your emotions all that be.
Whisper to me only those feelings so entirely.
Whisper me, whisper me, your love completely.

Callused Heart
by M. Griswold
04272020

A callused heart that is hard and strong.
From all the hurts that have done it wrong.
Concrete and anger now fills it's center spot.
With a soul that's tormented to molten hot.

Where is the love that is buried deep within?
Where is the caring passions to end or begin?
It would seem that all is hidden out of feeling.
So this heart has no hope of a tender healing.

How does one truely help such a callused heart.
Without tearing it in two and breaking it apart?
I am upon mine own heart's throbbing wits end.
To melt this heart I love that's so thick of skin.

Cuddling Caress
By M. Griswold
06272020

Cuddle close the one that loves you oh, so tender.
Hold softly to heart those emotions of this sender.
For they're passions that can never ever be bought
and come from one who's battles are hard won, fought.

Nestle near these words given in love so deep, freely.
Devour with understanding of heart their seedy mealy.
For they are the children of my pure, true loves want.
In hopes to be always treasured and never to flaunt.

Yearn with fever for my touches feel of gentle pressing.
Long with hope for my closeness's loves rich dressing.
Live for our love with a fire of desire's youthful zest.
For it offers you all of it's all in me, a true lover's rest.

My Loneliness
by M. Griswold
06242020

My loneliness inside, I cannot hide.
For you're my life, in you, I must abide.
When you're not near, my heart weeps to hear.
Your sweet, soft voice coming unto my ear.

This desire I feel is a fever that won't break.
It's terrible longing of a mournful soul ache.
My body trembles for a gentle, loving touch.
I want, I need only that you can give so much.

To whisper your name and hear only a echo.
My loneliness deepens, tears tumble then flow.
I reach in the night with a longing, lonely heart.
But you're not there, my hearts counterpart.

I dream of your return with every breath I take.
With visions of passions love, to you, I will make.
Holding on helplessly I await for only you.
No other love, no one else for me will truly do.

Loneliness, emptiness, all inside of me.
Dark is this space, heavy is it's company.
Your warm smile, I yearn to see evermore.
Chasing away shadows at love's front door.

My loneliness inside, I cannot hide.
For you are my life, in you, I must abide.
With patience and passion I do so yearn.
Awaiting patiently, in love, for your return.

by M. Griswold
071900

So teasable, irresistibly squeezable.
Cuddly and cute totally kissable.

Soft and warm, snuggling cozy.
With giggling charm, huggably rosy.

Unrelentingly tempting, compelling.
An essence of perfume, sweetly smelling.

These are the things so lovable about you.
That's why your so darn squeezable, through and through.

My Darling Fair
by M. Griswold
12272022

Oh sweet love, my darling fair,
hold me close and show you care.
Caress me in words of full affection.
Show our passion's true perfection.

Whisper "I love you" close to ear.
Coo it softly, as vapor, so I may hear.
Quivering under your love so bold,
is this faint heart that you now hold.

Within your arms I'm safe and free.
Bathing within a beauty of ecstasy.
No other place seems just and right,
shielded under our love this night.

If it be possible to forever remain,
held within this romantic plain.
Never to leave, never to say goodbye.
A true taste of heaven wherein I lie.

Oh sweet love, my darling fair,
hold me close and show your care.
For life without you being so near,
is a torture held within a lover's tear.

Love Is So Fickle
by M. Griswold
06242020

Love is so fickle of a passionate kind.
Tumbling the heart, confusing the mind.
Hormones soar, vision becomes blind.
Tentacles reaching in hope to bind.

Love is so fickle it twists and turns.
Searing the heart with boils and burns.
Indecisive in it's choices to release or hold.
Wavering decisions, am I hot or am I cold?

Loves is so fickle, oh yes, I am sorry to say.
For upon your lone heart it will feed one day.
With ravenous desires that refuse to wholly meld.
After all, humans are human and wish to be held.

My "If Only's"
by M. Griswold
07152020

If only I did what I should have learned to be done.
Maybe then I would've become my father's true son.

If only I had been more tolerant.
If only I had more reverent.
If only I had been more diligent.
If only I had not been so belligerent.

If only I had completed all that I had set out to do.
If only I loved only once, hated less than was due.
If only I said yes more often than no and or not.
If only I was satisfied with what exactly I got.

If only those things of which I once truly dreamed.
Had not been lost in the mist of my many schemes.
If only I had smelled more of life's bountiful scents,
I could have seen the world in a much better sense.

If only those people I used to know and love,
had not been grasped away by tragedies glove.
If only I had a second, third, or forth chance,
I'd cherish them all for relationships enhance.

If only time was as forgiving as a mothers gentle hand.
If only there was enough tempus to be at my command.
If only a moment would stand still within its rigid pace.
If only I had slowed in my greed's feverish race.

If only I had the real chance to do it all over again.
I don't think I'd change, no, not even one little sin.
For If I changed any of my "If Only's" you see.
I wouldn't be whom my "If Only's" led me to be.

Love's Value
by M. Griswold
07162020

What is the total value of a love that's true?
What does it mean, what's it's worth to you?
Would you be willing to invest some affection?
Would you be willing to risk a little rejection?

How would you view this love that's so true?
Could you tabulate its full worth's market value?
Will you be willing to mortgage your inner soul?
To invest in it's dreams, joys and hopes to know.

Why should you endow all of your whole heart?
In a love that may be doomed from the very start.
To besiege it so and then be able to lovingly let go.
Just for a chance at a chance of love to fully know.

Where is the sum of this love for you that's so true?
Would it's profits be shared totally by only two.
Can it's danger be totally minimized or maximized.
Could it be, would it be truly, really visualized.

When could you expect, realize its payment in full.
To reap its bounty, it's treasure of life's savings grow.
This love that is all consuming, so large and true.
What's all that mean, what's it all worth to you?

Loving Caress
By M. Griswold
08292020

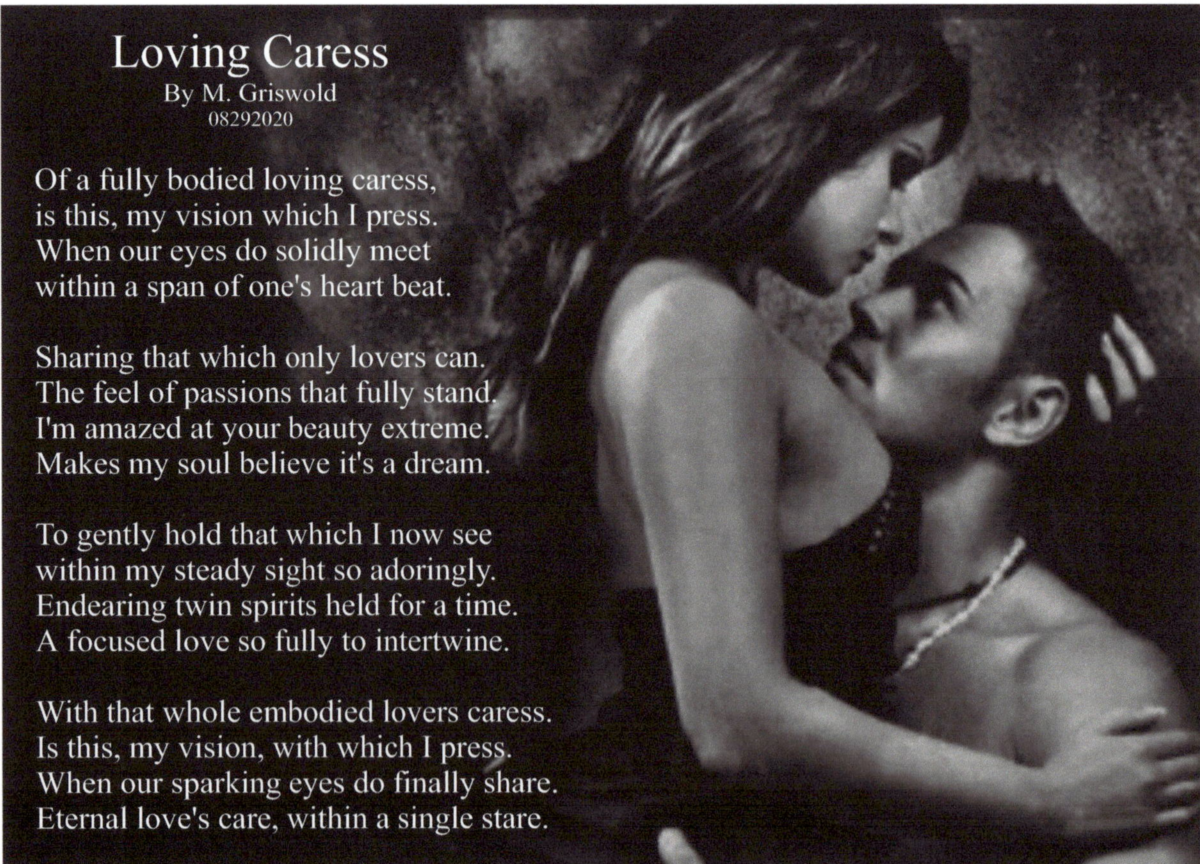

Of a fully bodied loving caress,
is this, my vision which I press.
When our eyes do solidly meet
within a span of one's heart beat.

Sharing that which only lovers can.
The feel of passions that fully stand.
I'm amazed at your beauty extreme.
Makes my soul believe it's a dream.

To gently hold that which I now see
within my steady sight so adoringly.
Endearing twin spirits held for a time.
A focused love so fully to intertwine.

With that whole embodied lovers caress.
Is this, my vision, with which I press.
When our sparking eyes do finally share.
Eternal love's care, within a single stare.

Magical Perplexity
by M. Griswold
06192020

Your a magical mystery which draws me near.
Can't place my finger on it, yet it is perfectly clear.
That twinkling in your eye, the warmth of your smile.
The grace of your form with such a beautiful style.

An attractive force which I just can't resist.
I am helpless in heart as the currents persist.
Driving me endlessly like a moth to a flame.
Your spirit does entrance me, direct in it's aim.

Why so captive am I that I am a ponder to understand.
Never have I been under such a magical command.
Demanding my affections to which I voluntarily give.
For it seems now without you I surely wouldn't live.

Beautiful sorcery to which I haven't any self control.
Of primal surge passionate does it lustfully grow.
Your magical mystery of soulful, wrenching harmony.
Is wonderfully quizzical, mystical in it's perplexity.

Sweet Words

By M. Griswold
07082022

Speak to me sweet words of a romantic kind.
Reach deep within our love to which we bind.
Then gently touch passions with soothing verbs.
Of a type that excites like scent ripened herbs.

Declarations streaming whispered softly to me.
Ones of great power voiced in loving honesty.
Utterances transmitted through moist soft lips.
Words of a rose blossom's bloom dew that drips.

This is what I need to feed my feelings desire.
Igniting this soul with adoring, torrid fire.
A kind of moist candy to sweeten my spirit.
Craving, I tremble and quiver just to hear it.

With a pen of passion, sketch me loves art.
Pressing fragrant oaths upon this panting heart.
Inform me gently with lettered promises true.
From the depths of your being fully through.

Speak to me sweet words from your loving chest.
Breathless, I lay under them to caress me to rest.
Please speak forever of your love's rich reflection.
From your heart, these words of sweet affection.

Why I love
by M. Griswold
07172020

Grace, beauty, intelligence and more
are those elements in you that I adore.

The time and patience that you apply to me.
That willingness to accept just who you see.

The caring heart with your passionate press.
That twinkle in your eye when you say yes.

All these things are why I love you so much.
And that's why I need your tender, loving touch.

For I love that true full woman that you are.
From your beginning to end, from near or far.

Dissolving
by M. Griswold
04282020

I don't understand her.
She doesn't understand me.
Without understanding,
   how can love be.

I want to show passion,
   she laughs at me.
   I want to be close,
      but she pushes away.

   I want to love her fully,
      she shuns me completely.
   Who is this woman
      whom I love whole heartedly?

      I am confused in my commitment,
      she is steadfast in herself only.
      How is it possible to stay involved
         when a relationship has all dissolved.

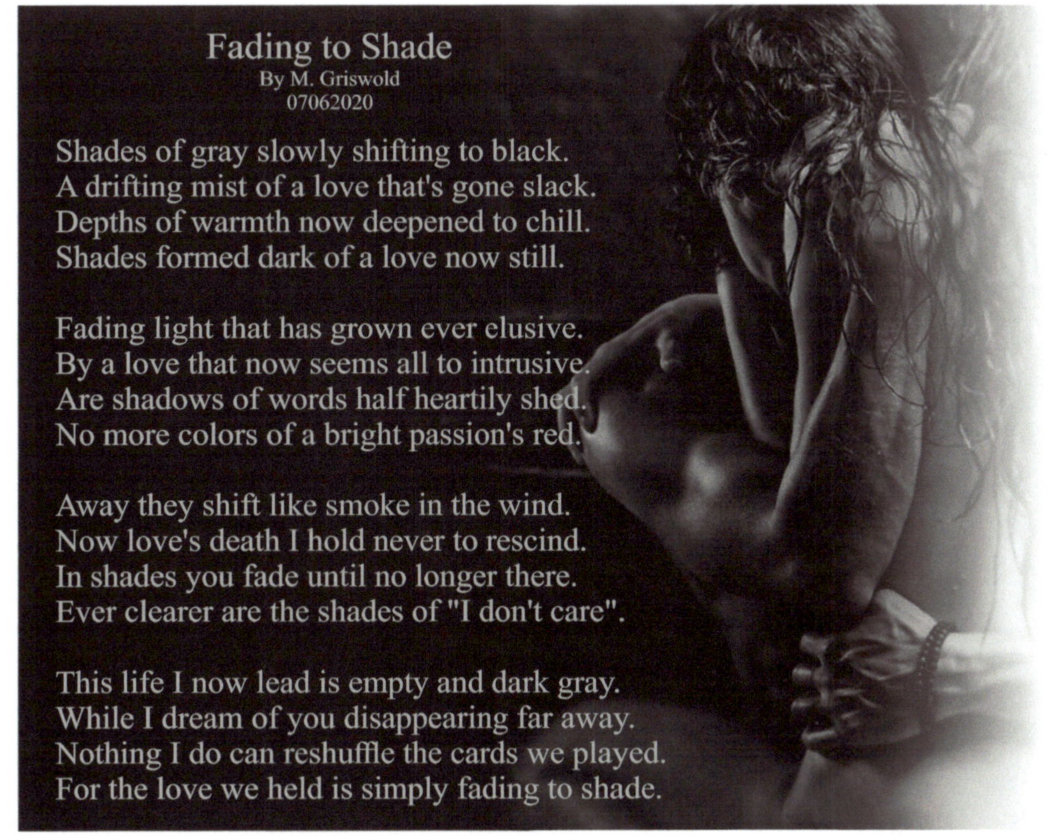

Fading to Shade
By M. Griswold
07062020

Shades of gray slowly shifting to black.
A drifting mist of a love that's gone slack.
Depths of warmth now deepened to chill.
Shades formed dark of a love now still.

Fading light that has grown ever elusive.
By a love that now seems all to intrusive.
Are shadows of words half heartily shed.
No more colors of a bright passion's red.

Away they shift like smoke in the wind.
Now love's death I hold never to rescind.
In shades you fade until no longer there.
Ever clearer are the shades of "I don't care".

This life I now lead is empty and dark gray.
While I dream of you disappearing far away.
Nothing I do can reshuffle the cards we played.
For the love we held is simply fading to shade.

My Weeping Heart

by M. Griswold
06092020

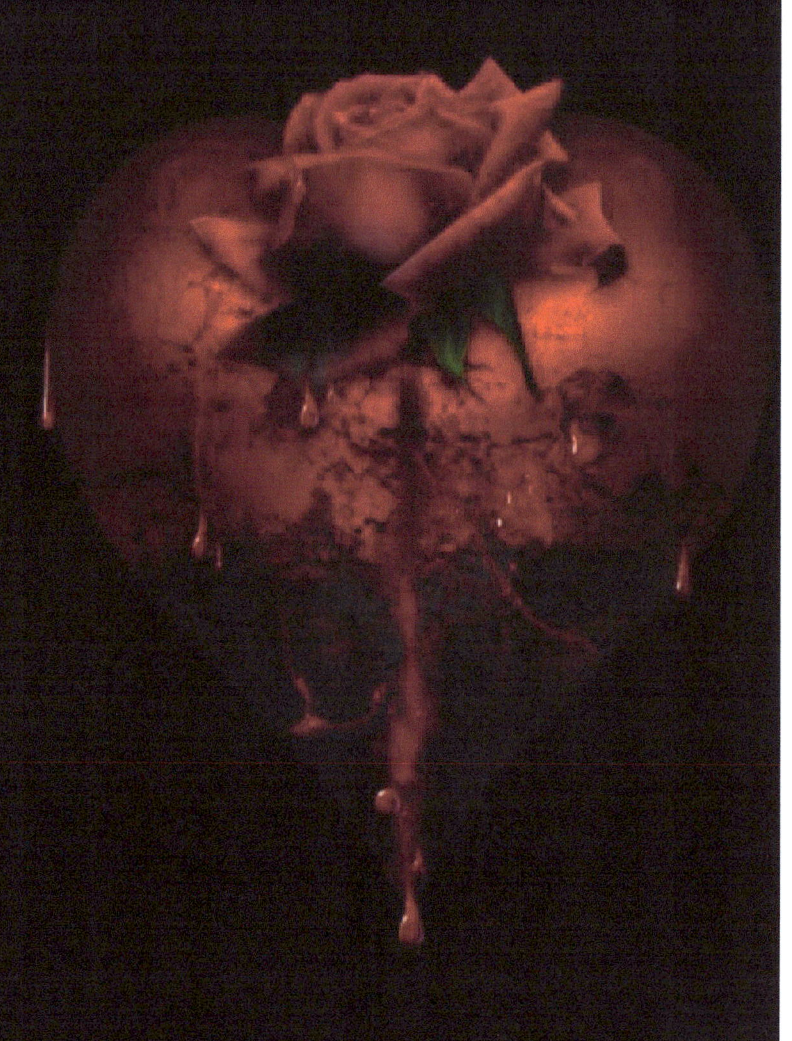

Oh weeping heart quite your sobbing tears
as I draw you close and hold you near.
For I know you are sad for loneliness's sake
so let me dry those droplets you make.
Calm yourself to patience side
and allow me to ebb your passions tide.

Yes, it has been a long journey of sorrow
dark nights with shadows dim and hollow.
Many solitary times when you seem all alone
and no one near to call your own.
Loneliness is but a dark abyss
that drinks it's fill of your fluid's sweet kiss.

Dreaming a dream of fullness's breath
then awaking to morrow's empty depths.
Those moments hard of longing's sorrow.
Greater still is believing in a tomorrow.
I understand that hollow, empty echo's cry,
the one in which your tears fallen now lie.

Weep if you must, sob if your need,
for I your spirit, upon those seeds do feed.
Gathering in those drops that have fallen,
those little bits of life's harshest pollen.
To grow you up and make you strong.
For you are my passion and I'm your song.

You Are

by M. Griswold
07052022R1

You are like a blooming radiant sunrise.
A breath of morning freshness to realize.

You are that smile which passes these lips.
When your vision, my eyes focus on, then grips.

You are all seasons, from summer to spring.
A humming harmony that allows birds to sing.

You are the beating of a song's passion rhythm.
It's beginning to it's end and all that's therein.

You are my constant love, the whole of my life.
Of endless days of light with little or no strife.

You are totally fullness to me, within it's all in all.
For you, I will live and love 'til death's final call.

"

For Her Pleasure

By M. Griswold
07132020

The evening is cool and moisture laden.
As I lay naked beside this lovely maiden.
Illuminated only by a candles flicker glow.
Shadows dancing to our heated fevers flow.

Her beauty radiant in the half darkened night.
I, aflame in my passion at her glistening sight.
To touch, to caress, I anxiously tremble to know.
With expectations of coursing desires interior flow.

Gently, trembling, I kiss her form bare lying just so.
Taking care, moving slow, she lightly quivers as I go.
Breath quickens, breast ascending, nipples hard arise.
Pink flesh is silk under my roving touch to tantalize.

Nibbling ear, kissing neck, licking stomach to thigh.
Leaving not one choice of measure untouched, do I.
Searching, probing to find her sensual warm spot.
I then, chase to attain our love, enriching it to hot.

She raises to me in her full ecstasies ultimate desire.
Pressing me inward to release those juice's lit afire.
Sweet nectar erupts as currents ooze then flow forth.
Continuing, I ensue completion of her pleasure's course.

Bodies rise and then descend, shadows dance to transcend.
Total commitment to her heated emotions stead I attend.
Passions now concluding of an evenings torrid love's end.
For her pleasure in this, to toil within her cravings I tend.

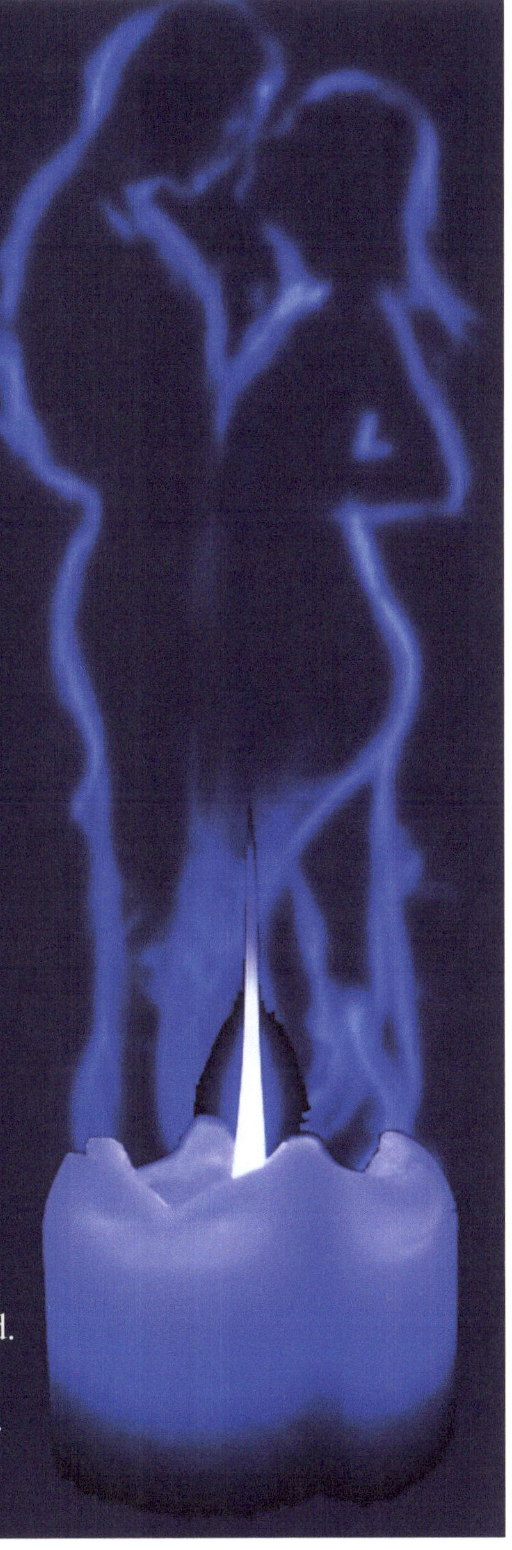

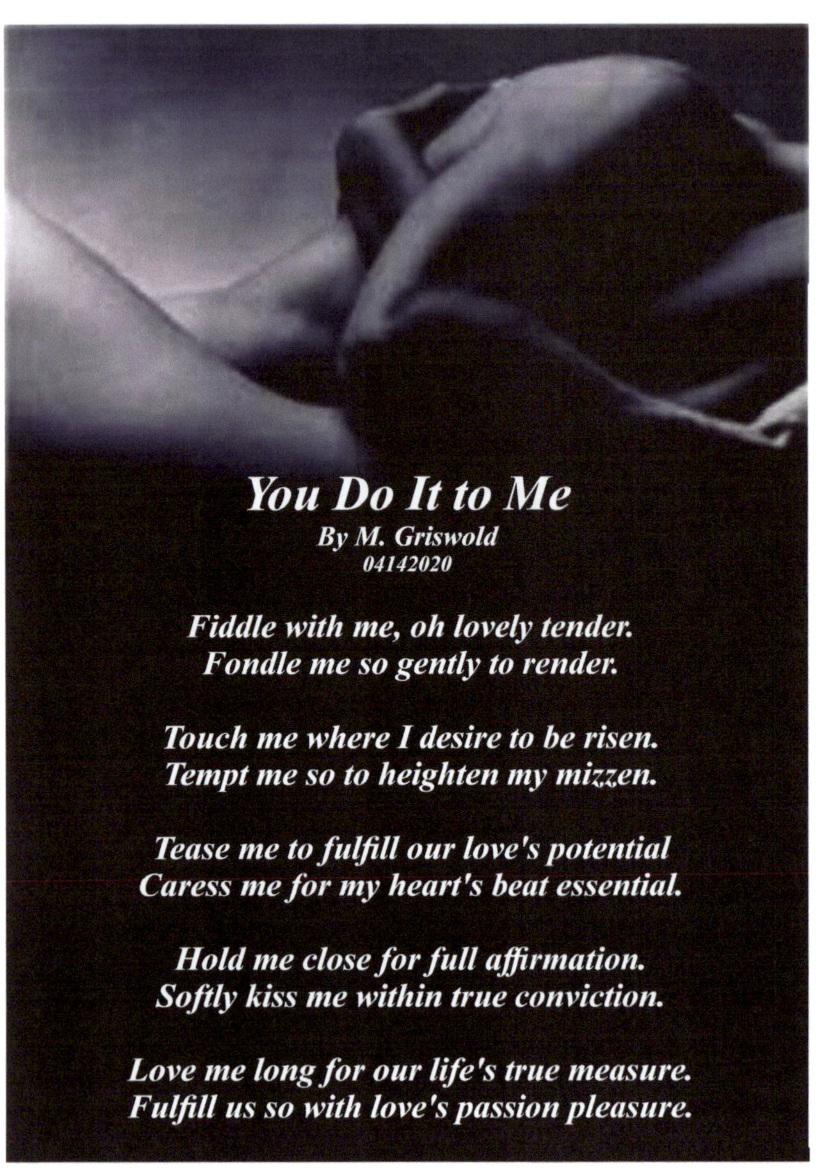

You Do It to Me
By M. Griswold
04142020

Fiddle with me, oh lovely tender.
Fondle me so gently to render.

Touch me where I desire to be risen.
Tempt me so to heighten my mizzen.

Tease me to fulfill our love's potential
Caress me for my heart's beat essential.

Hold me close for full affirmation.
Softly kiss me within true conviction.

Love me long for our life's true measure.
Fulfill us so with love's passion pleasure.

Sands of Love
by M. Griswold
07012020

Twin measures of sand held within hands
to gauge how love can longingly stand.

The left cupped gentle to hold so lightly.
The right gripped boldly, far too tightly.

One pile tenderly supported with loving care.
It's granules shift, but are still carefully there.

The second having been squeezed with force,
displaced and drained with no love's discourse.

The left hand now with it's sand rich and full.
The other is completely empty, no love to know.

Would You Miss Me
By M. Griswold
04132020

Would you miss me if I didn't call.
Would you miss me, miss me at all.
Would you care if I wasn't even there.
Would you miss all the love we share.

My soft gentle touch, would you miss.
My Tender sweet words of passion's bliss.
A loving caress from me would you miss.
Or even care for the absence of my kiss.

Would you feel empty from the lack of me.
Would you experience a hollow heart's frailty.
Would you wear a smile or a longing frown.
Would you miss me if I just wasn't around.

I wonder, I ponder in questioning reflections.
Only because of your seeming lack of affections.
Would you miss my loving attentions ever so small.
Would you miss me, miss me even a little at all.

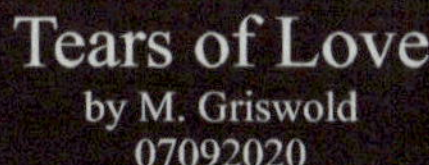

Tears of Love
by M. Griswold
07092020

Tears of love have, to me, come once again.
This heart's given into passion's grip of pain.
Flowing from my very soul's center herein.
Streaming down in currents upon this skin.

The waters of love from this tormented soul.
Of cascading emotions that were out of control.
A Love held captive within his selfish desire.
Hoping, just one more time for a love to inspire.

But this time my tears returned as cold rains.
With no chance for an apologies lying stains.
Far too many times the pain has been applied.
The respect I had once has now surely died.

The tears of remorse will now stain his face.
He now will know of a lover's wrath in place.
I shall never again allow tears to so easily fall.
For one holding a lustful heart to touch me at all.

Showering Torrents

by M. Griswold
09262020

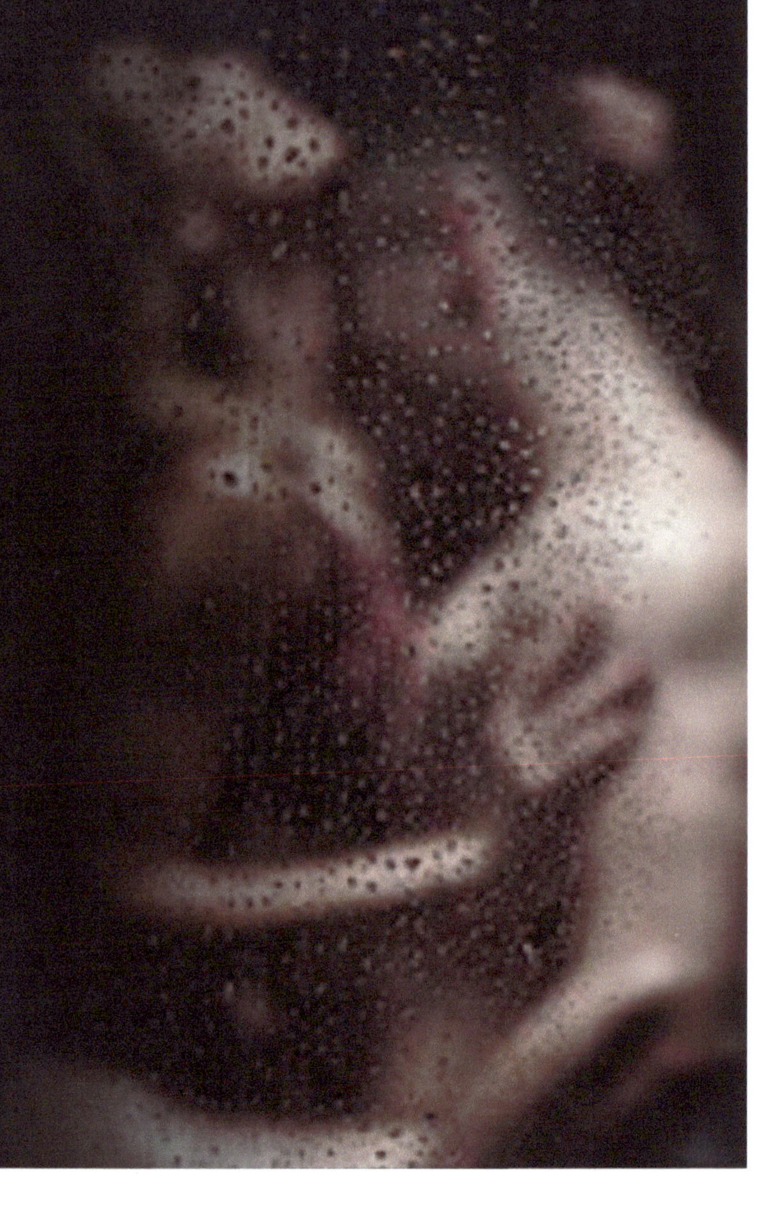

Soothing strokes of lathered hands press.
Upon skin moistened by hot showers dress.
Streaming down soft naked flesh, steaming.
Rinsed by lover's luscious licks, careening.

Forms shiver under the heated currents pour.
Washing one another to then tenderly explore.
Finding hidden spots of pleasures fully gained.
Rippling to tremble under warmness attained.

Kissing under the cascading heated waters flow.
Fondling teasing tongues, touching licking slow.
Passion dances between coursing water powered.
As the liquid blends in this torrid love devoured.

Sensing the fluid flowing like sweet pure rain.
Channeling in waves like bubbling champagne.
Curtains of wetness encompass us in and about.
Drenching twin figures both fully inside and out.

Fondly toweling of those dripping, moist places.
Sensitive to dabble dry those affectionate spaces.
Soaking to sponge any loosened tangled warrants.
Wrapped in the warmth of a showers wet torrents.

Oh, the freshness of a hot, heated shower shared.
Its warmth rising mixture of a loves vapors bared.
A romantic encounter of our nakedness to address.
By showering torrents of a hearts steaming caress.

Tears Of Loves Yearning

By M. Griswold
08292020

My yearning heart weeps slowly, silently in persist.
For a love found but yet, is elusive within life's mist.

Within her grace of beauty I reach for her longing.
But she teasingly is aloof from her own belonging.

Invisible tears stream dryly as to gently wet my soul.
Never ceasing, never easing, this love weeps to know.

When will this imprisonment end so my heart can sing.
When will I yearn no longer for this loves beating ring.

My heart cries silently, with dry tears of loves yearning.

I Wanna Get Drunk
by M. Griswold
03312020

I wanna get drunk, drunk with our loves spirit.
Slobber'in, stink'in, fall'in down, roll'in round lit.
Bubble'in over, dripping down, and fully wet.
That's how stink'in drunk I wanna really get.

Ta drink ya in like sweet bourbon on the rocks.
Burp ya up some ta cause a love'in vapor lock.
No on the wagon fer me, no quit'in fer me, no sir'ree.
I'm a tea totaling volunteer and intoxicated to easily.

Guzzle ya down to fill this staggering heart fully up.
Trouble is, there's never enough of ya within ma cup.
A bottomless glass of sweet ecstasy is all that I need.
I can never drink enough of yur passions rich feed.

Let me be a wino and a drunk on one bended knee.
Begg'in fer love would be ma wishful longings plea.
I just wanna get drunk on yur lov'in spirits flow.
All of ya, all of ya, down the hatch ya'd lov'inly go.

My Gift to You
by M. Griswold
07032020

To speak to you of thoughts that I hold.
Would be of me that which is too bold.
I want to say that it's you that I yearn.
So dear to my heart my love does burn.

These words are true, all of them for you.
To hold you close is my desire's true hue.
To touch your soft hair, to kiss and caress.
So gentle I'd be within my passion's press.

For into you lovingly would I give to release.
The knowledge of my joy's emotions of peace.
With love so tender I would give you my words.
So as to understand the meaning of these verbs.

To hold in my arms your lovely warm presence.
To bask in your smiles laughing rich essence.
To look into your deep eyes and speak of love.
To whisper sweet words like a soft flying dove.

To sweep you from your feet, I jealously desire.
And quench in you this heat of my passion's fire.
To fill you up of what dreams are truly made of.
This would be the gift I give, my heart's true love.

Tell Me How Much You Love Me

By M. Griswold
12171999

Tell me how much you love me.
Until the birds sing no more.
Tell me how much you love me.
To the horizon's distant shore.

Tell me how much you love me.
Until the Winter becomes the Spring.
Tell me how much you love me.
To the end of everything.

Tell me how much you love me.
Until my love comes home again.
Tell me how much you love me.
From the beginning unto the end.

To tell me how much you love you.
Is to bare my inner soul.
To tell you how much I love you.
Is to know us being whole.

True Beauty

by M. Griswold
06262020

Thine beauty true lies in the depths within.
Take little heed of the package that it's in.
A persons real value is stored in one's heart.
Not in the physical appearance of fleshly art.

Those who judge only of an outward glance.
Are missing the real treasure of a chance.
To meet true elegance in it's full splendor.
Of seeing you in your true beauty rendered.

I Want a Divorce
by M. Griswold
06132020

I want a divorce and I want it right now.
I can't live with you anymore, anyhow.
My life is in torment from loving you.
It's like loving a rock that said I do.

Your heart is as cold as cold can be.
Like living in Winter's deep frigidity.
No emotions come, no passions to bare.
Only anger's curse is what you now share.

It takes two to make a marriage grow strong.
To create a love that will last a full life long.
But I stand here now with a sad, broken heart.
One that you've seen fit to rip and tear all apart.

I've tried my best to love you where you were.
But it just wasn't enough for your heart to stir.
I knew it when I married you and ignored it so.
That little small voice in me that shouted "NO"!

How can God expect us to live like this.
A commitment of love that went far amiss.
You've made my life a little Hell on Earth.
I given more to this marriage than it's worth.

No time to waste, I can't take another minute.
I want my life back in full without you in it.
Let's see a lawyer and break this stale vow.
I want a divorce and I want it right now!

Tickle Me Blue

by M. Griswold
03192020

Tickle me blue if you would fully so please.
For this is how I need for you to me tease.
A form of love that shows that you really care.
Finding those spots so funny and tender share.

Tickle me blue if you so openly do choose.
Titillate my feet without any socks or shoes.
Make my toes wiggle and crazy squirm.
Touching me gentle and yet, never to firm.

Tickle me blue without any chance of release.
Give me slow no quarter, give me no real peace.
Take me to the limits until my laughter's insane.
Fondle me completely until I am out of my brain.

Tickle me blue until I don't know what to do.
Then hold me close and kiss me soulfully true.
Hug me long and strong passionately through.
But please don't ever stop tickling me blue.

Twilight Passions

by M. Griswold
071800

Twinkling twilight, early summer breeze.
Dimming dull dusk, a setting sun flees.
Moon rising, gaining radiance in shine.
Loves ember glowing, lunar tides climb.

Passions bliss glistening, two lovers kiss.
Hearts opened full to a summer nights wish.
Huddled together clutching, darkness gleams.
Forever souls touch, joined spirits in streams.

Silhouettes dark upon a stage of gentle slope.
Soft forms entwined unto a heavenly hope.
Nothing else matters, everything else bared.
Only this place, only this time, now shared.

Love blooms to flower in this eves afterset.
Stars glowing within both in circles pirouette.
Attaining heights of loves plateaus to attain.
Where tonight's twilight passion to ever reign.

The Sweetest Piece of Candy

by M. Griswold
09052020

You're the sweetest piece of candy that's ever crossed my lips.
Your confection is perfection like chocolate richly drips.
A morsel of tasty pastry that's freshly warm, delicious.
A mouth watering delight, of a lovable spice tantalus.

Never before nor ever again, will I eat a more delectable flavor
than your full abundance's essence, a treat pleasing savor.
Teasing, pleasing, fully salivary gland squeezing,
mouth watering juices flowing with obscenities pleasing.

Oh, fragrant treat to my tongues wanting taste buds.
Sample me give, of your brown, rich bodies flood.
For never before nor ever again,
will I taste a sweeter piece of candied sin.

Sweet Whispers

By M. Griswold
12312022

Kissably soft, moist fully rendered,
are whispered words lovingly tendered.
With spoken passion and desires that be
your smooth voice echoes through eternity.

No other can do it, no other but you,
touches this heart in the way you do.
Gentle offerings in love's warm blindness,
shows me a touchable, true, pure kindness.

Whispered in that yearning, loving tone,
from lips so sweet, inviting me, come home.
Whispers that can melt a hard soul's center.
It beckons me on, within our love to enter.

Please, never stop uttering soft sounds to me.
Those reminders of love's care given, tenderly.
For I need to hear them, I desire them so.
Those sweet whispers of your voice to know.

Return to My Heart
by M. Griswold
08312020

So very far from home and I'm all alone.
My heart's sadder by every beating tone.

The heaviness that I feel will not depart
until I return to you, keeper of my heart.

Yearning constantly for that which I left.
A love so treasured which is now bereft.

How can I survive this horrid emptiness
without feeling your soft, sweet caress.

I cry in the night and weep within the day.
A full bodied circle of a tear filled bouquet.

Tortured so, I work towards my ends goal.
To return to you, the caretaker of my soul.

Far from your arms and so terribly alone.
Take care of my heart, until I return home.

Slow Loving
by M. Griswold
06272020

Sifting though your every space with gestures of my passions grace.
Lightly, with fingers lightly soft, I trace impressions upon your face.
Giving you my tenderness touching, fully relaxed within their due.
Loving slowly, deeply, is this hearts passionate desire for all of you.

From Sundown to Sunrise there is no less amount that I wholly give.
To make these, our emotions, last forever and a day within us to live.
A torrid flame that slowly burns bright to grow now and evermore.
Slow loving, from out of my heart always sending, unending to pour.

Caressing word offered lightly and honestly in heated whisper's kind.
Gradual motions of my love's pressing verbs that lovingly will us bind.
Breath upon breast to moisten and flow into your beautiful, loving heart.
Slow loving fantasies pleasures I labor constantly to pleasingly impart.

Loving you diligently, forever is this, my soul's passion, for your being.
Longing to apply soothing pantomimes of my love's depth true feeling.
Taking much time so I may drink of all your richness and grace full in.
This, my gentle slow loving, focused and committed to you I will attend.

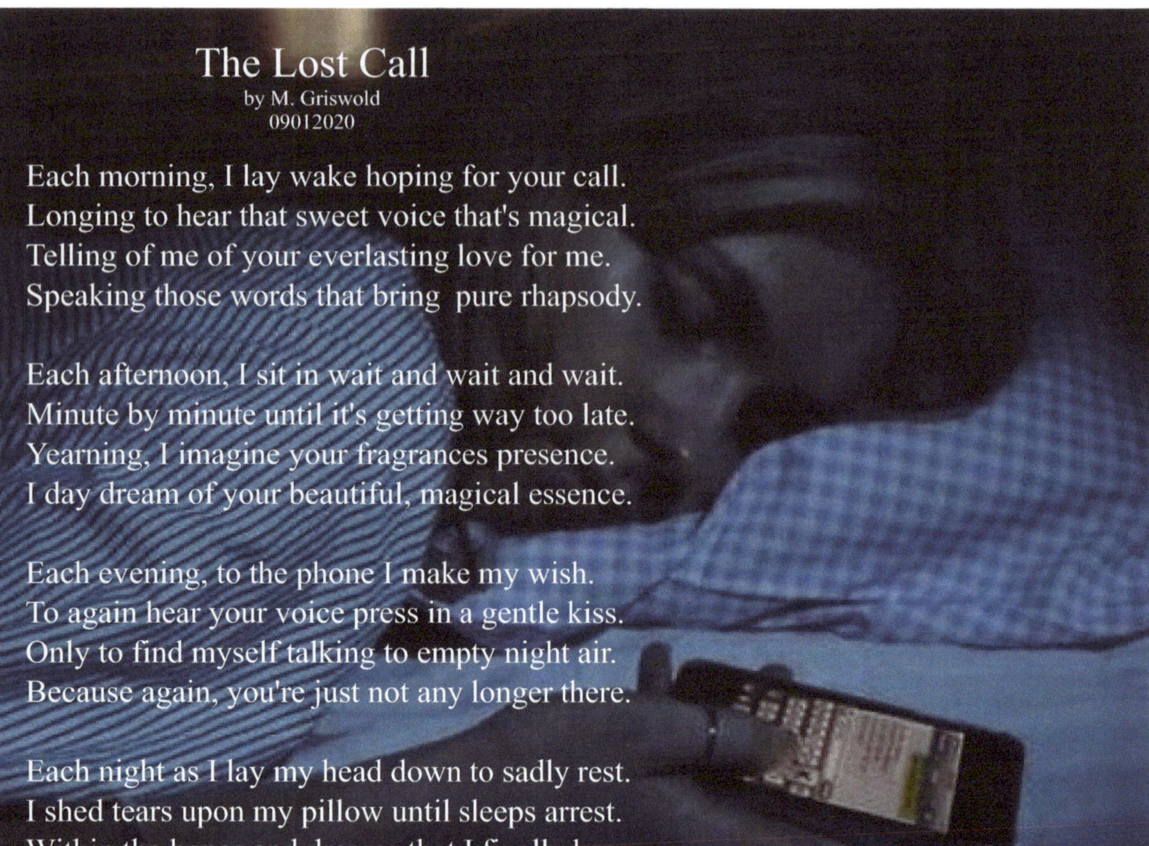

The Lost Call
by M. Griswold
09012020

Each morning, I lay wake hoping for your call.
Longing to hear that sweet voice that's magical.
Telling of me of your everlasting love for me.
Speaking those words that bring pure rhapsody.

Each afternoon, I sit in wait and wait and wait.
Minute by minute until it's getting way too late.
Yearning, I imagine your fragrances presence.
I day dream of your beautiful, magical essence.

Each evening, to the phone I make my wish.
To again hear your voice press in a gentle kiss.
Only to find myself talking to empty night air.
Because again, you're just not any longer there.

Each night as I lay my head down to sadly rest.
I shed tears upon my pillow until sleeps arrest.
Within the hopes and dreams that I finally hear.
That lost call from you that never, ever appeared.

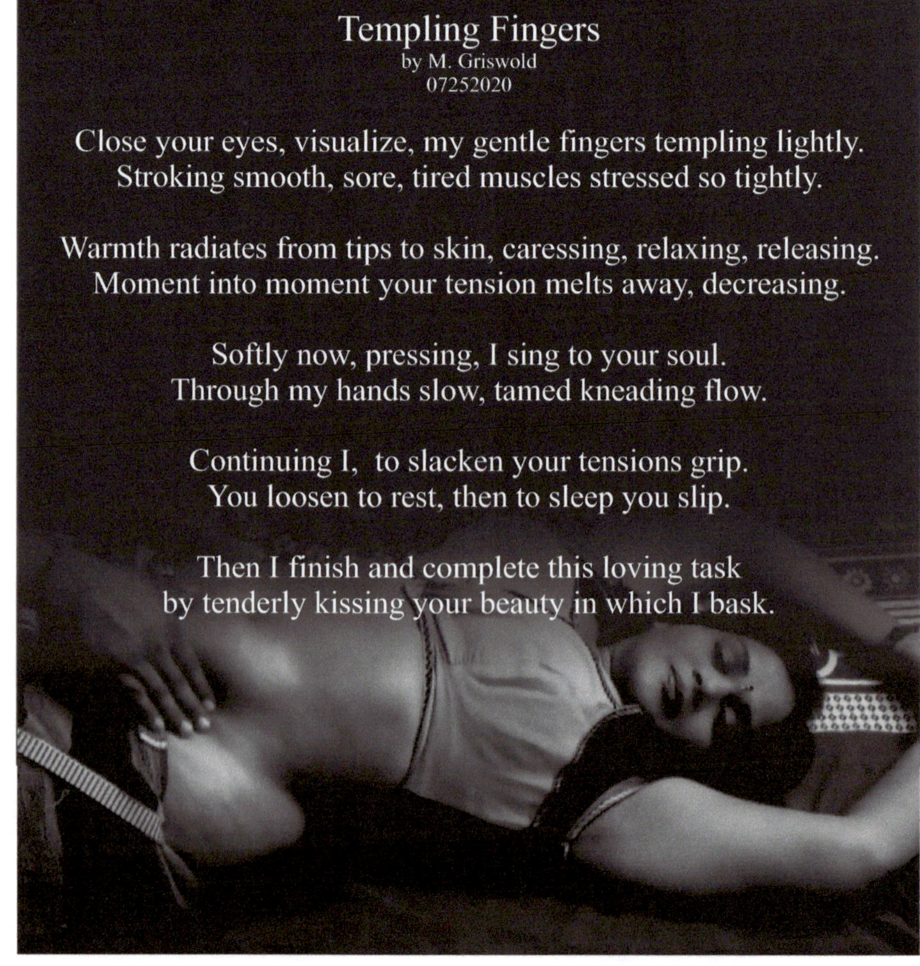

Templing Fingers
by M. Griswold
07252020

Close your eyes, visualize, my gentle fingers templing lightly.
Stroking smooth, sore, tired muscles stressed so tightly.

Warmth radiates from tips to skin, caressing, relaxing, releasing.
Moment into moment your tension melts away, decreasing.

Softly now, pressing, I sing to your soul.
Through my hands slow, tamed kneading flow.

Continuing I, to slacken your tensions grip.
You loosen to rest, then to sleep you slip.

Then I finish and complete this loving task
by tenderly kissing your beauty in which I bask.

Why It Won't Work Again
by M. Griswold
07022020

Needing to know why it won't work again.
This love, our love, to which we were in.
I read these words I've bared from my heart.
So as to remind me never again, forever apart.

What once was a true love shared by two.
Now is empty, a deep reaching abyss of blue.
Hollowed of all passion, our romance stolen.
This heart now bruised and bleeding, swollen.

Of many memories trodden in life's muddy path.
A silence that echos against barren angers wrath.
Of a roller coaster ride many times twisted, slides.
Where no similar interests and boredom resides.

As I read, I realize, why it won't work ever again.
Releasing you now so we may let healing begin.
Forgiving all, to openly love once more and give.
This I must focus on to begin again to fully live.

One Sided Love
by M. Griswold
07222020

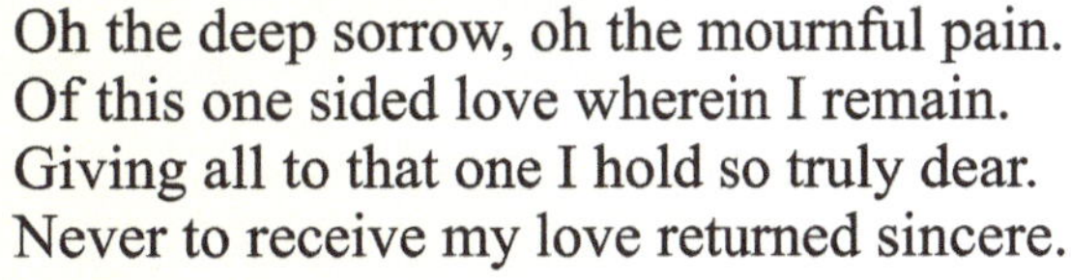

Oh the deep sorrow, oh the mournful pain.
Of this one sided love wherein I remain.
Giving all to that one I hold so truly dear.
Never to receive my love returned sincere.

The joy has gone, its innocents has left.
All that tides in and out is a heart bereft.
Hard love holding, it has to be enduring.
Foolish passions hanging in there strong.

I have no a choice, this matter of my heart.
Your essence has me captive in every part.
A willing servant complete, in love and life.
Ignoring your ignoring, I continue my strife.

Just once to be shown from the one I love.
To feel those affections reflections thereof.
To know my heart is truly returned in kind.
Not one sided but doubled so for us to bind.

Oh the deep sorrow, oh the mournful pain.
Of this one sided love wherein I remain.
Giving all to that one I hold so truly dear.
My love is wasted on one whom is insincere.

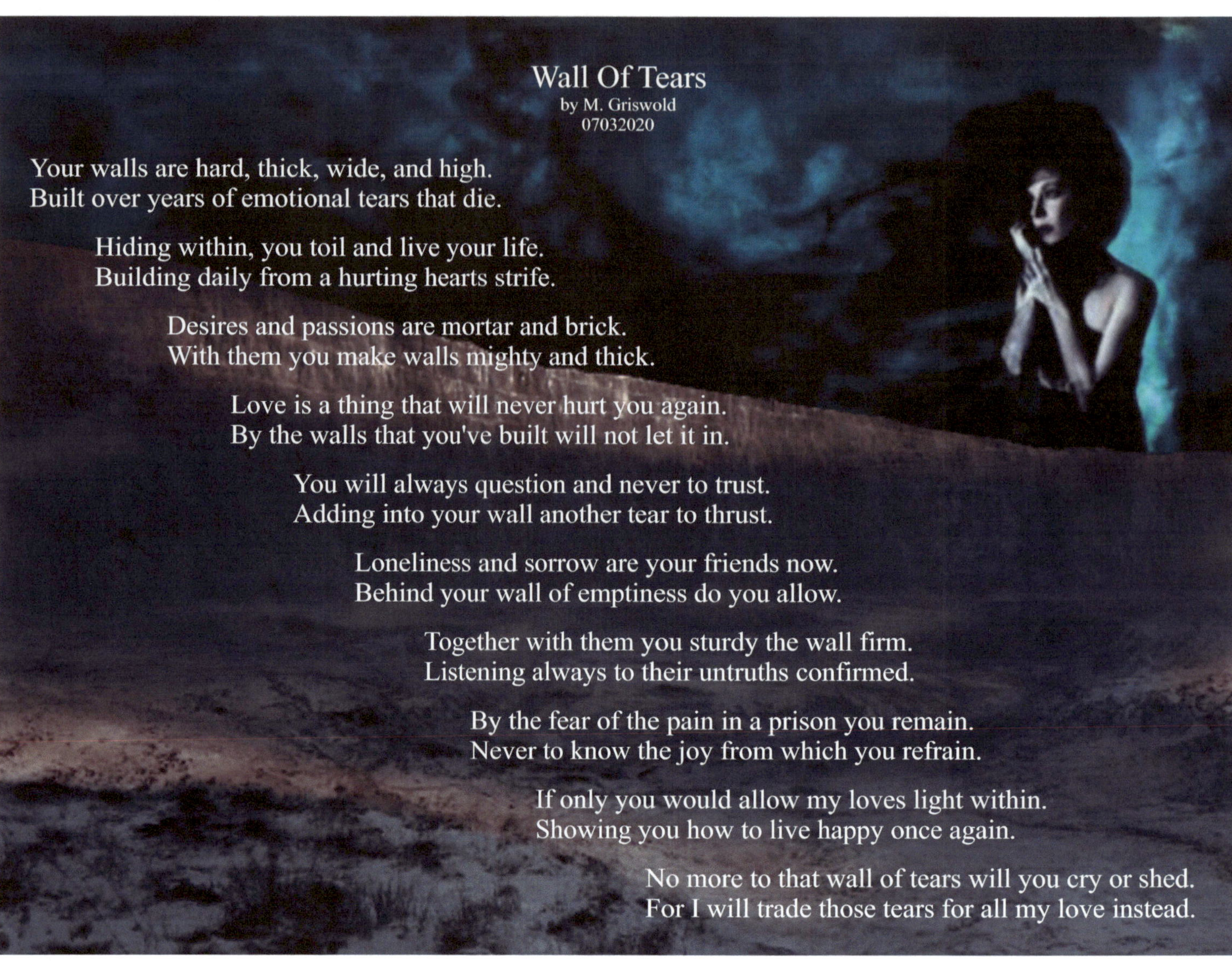

Wall Of Tears
by M. Griswold
07032020

Your walls are hard, thick, wide, and high.
Built over years of emotional tears that die.

Hiding within, you toil and live your life.
Building daily from a hurting hearts strife.

Desires and passions are mortar and brick.
With them you make walls mighty and thick.

Love is a thing that will never hurt you again.
By the walls that you've built will not let it in.

You will always question and never to trust.
Adding into your wall another tear to thrust.

Loneliness and sorrow are your friends now.
Behind your wall of emptiness do you allow.

Together with them you sturdy the wall firm.
Listening always to their untruths confirmed.

By the fear of the pain in a prison you remain.
Never to know the joy from which you refrain.

If only you would allow my loves light within.
Showing you how to live happy once again.

No more to that wall of tears will you cry or shed.
For I will trade those tears for all my love instead.

My Squeeze'ums
By M. Griswold
05032020

My squeeze'ums is squeezable most of the time.
Lovable and hugable, truly cuddling divine.
Like a stuffed toy, she's puffy, fluffy and cute.
I love my squeeze'ums clean down to her root.

My squeeze'ums is warm and soft to the touch.
Teasable, ticklable, smoochable oh, so very much.
Likeable, laughable, wholly jolly with mirth.
She has a smile that's a million bucks worth.

So how do I know that my squeeze'ums really mine?
By the twinkle in her eye and a kiss returned in kind.
And when I squeeze my squeeze'ums like a maniac.
My squeeze'ums squeezes me fully, lovingly right back.

Yearning Embrace

by M. Griswold
07202020

My soul yearns for your embrace.
A soft tender kiss placed upon my face.

I need you now like never before.
My being is open, please come explore.

Feelings I thought that had long been dead.
All back again racing, raging in my head.

My soul yearns for your embrace.
A soft tender kiss placed upon my face.

How can I explain the want, the desire.
That's ablaze in my heart, a lonely fire.

Never to hurt and only to love.
Feelings surely come from above.

My soul yearns for your embrace.
A soft tender kiss placed upon my face.

I am so scared to let this all be true.
A fantasy, a fiction, my emotions for you.

I must control these passions I've gained.
Or surely I will go totally, completely insane.

My soul yearns for your embrace.
A soft tender kiss placed upon my face.

It's such a distance between you and me.
Our spirits touch but no holding can be.

Maybe in the future our paths will cross.
Two souls meeting with hopes to emboss.

My soul yearns for your embrace.
A soft tender kiss placed upon my face.

The Need In Me
By M. Griswold
07022020

There's a need in me for my love to feed.
For anyone who cares and take it's seed.
Then, to return unto this lonely soul
the love I desire to desperately know.

Any heart that will accept without question
that which is me within true loves affection.
Another spirit that yearns for my essence.
To share always in loves lasting presence.

Many games have been played with this heart.
Where love has been shattered, broken apart.
Ripped from it's depths for unfeeling pleasures
by those wishing to steal of it's hidden treasures.

This need in me won't be quenched by games.
For I desire a love with everlasting hot flames.
Of a passion that lives and is returned in true.
One that can only be honestly enriched by two.

Two giving all within a love deep and rich.
With a desire that's passionately wholly stitched.
Taking away fully this feeling of a need in me.
For it never to return in it's saddened sincerity.

Tormented Love
By M. Griswold
12012021

Why, oh why, do I torment myself so?
Opening emotions then letting them go.
When it's apparent that you toy with me.
Teasing to play with my feelings so openly.

I am truly earnest within my loving of you.
Why can't you do the same and be honest too?
But you pull on my passions, this way and that.
Abusing my heart like an old dusty floor mat.

Why, oh why, do I reveal my soul full, completely?
Letting it's guard down, beckoning you on, sweetly.
Unconditionally, I accept your caring attentions.
Ignoring all, for love's sake, your true intentions.

Why, oh why, you're playing these games with me?
Am I so ignorant and dumb, or just don't want to see?
Overlooking those things that I choose to withstand.
Only to have you love me from the back of your hand.

Sweet Honey

by M. Griswold
07132020

Honey, sweet, slowly dripping.
From out of your hive, love is gripping.
Thickly rich, promising always to deliver
a steaming flavor that makes me quiver.

To bite, to taste of your readied comb.
Licking it's fullness of your volumes tome.
To probe and prod into a full nest to invest.
My stinger now harvests your honey's best.

Mmmm, lip smacking, tongue twisting.
Raw temptation, there is no resisting.
Stickyness flowing, your nectar teases me.
Inward, onward, buzzing this busy little bee.

I must have you, to your last drops drew.
Pleasure is my want from you to pursue.
Nothing will satisfy this sensual craving.
Of a sweet honey's tasting that's enslaving.

Your Beauty Makes Me Nervous

by M. Griswold
04122020

Your beauty makes me nervous in a very special way.
Speech grows deadly silent for forgetting what to say.
When your eyes meet mine my breath is whisped away.
Your beauty holds me captive in dumbfounded display.

Your beauty make me shy in bashful sheepish play.
To much the red upon my cheeks, emotions do betray.
When you smile it's as if the night turns suddenly to day.
The warmth of your presents is a flower turned bouguet.

I don't know how to approach for my shyness does weigh.
So I write this pitiful letter of a nervous heart's dismay.
I dare not believe or think so in my selfishness I pray.
Such beauty as yours would have time for me someday.

Your beauty makes me nervous in a very beautiful special way.
I lose all that I am within your presents, my heart stolen away.
I wish that I wasn't so nervous and be so boldly brave to say,
"Would you come out with me for a cup coffee or tea today?"

To This Garden

By M. Griswold
07112020

To this garden I will feed and tend.
Without ceasing, without any end.
Toiling ever in love's sweet labor.
Minding not of sacrifice's ill flavor.

Daily, I will pluck out unwanted weeds.
Then gently caress the newborn seeds.
Watering and pampering their every need.
To maturity I, this garden, will always feed.

Weathering storms of darkened skies.
Shielding the winds of wilting demise.
Protecting always this garden's pure flower.
Armored with love's full blooming power.

For it's our future, this garden, you see.
Our dreams, our wishes, our rhapsody.
To this garden of love, I will attend.
Without ceasing, without any end.

Stream of Dreams
by M. Griswold
07082020

To dream of my dreams
then to explore their means
of loving you to all extremes.
Is my fantasy of erotic streams.

To feel those means
I explore within my extremes.
Then to excite those streams.
Of my love, I see within my dreams.

Currents flowing to their extremes.
Now that I'm swimming inside the streams.
As gently, I lay upon you within my dreams.
Pleasures ecstasy erupts by your your means.

All my colors explode to fully brilliant streams.
Trembling passions are now of rippling dreams.
Shivers this soul by your caressing calming means.
Of love making dreams that's are taken to extremes.

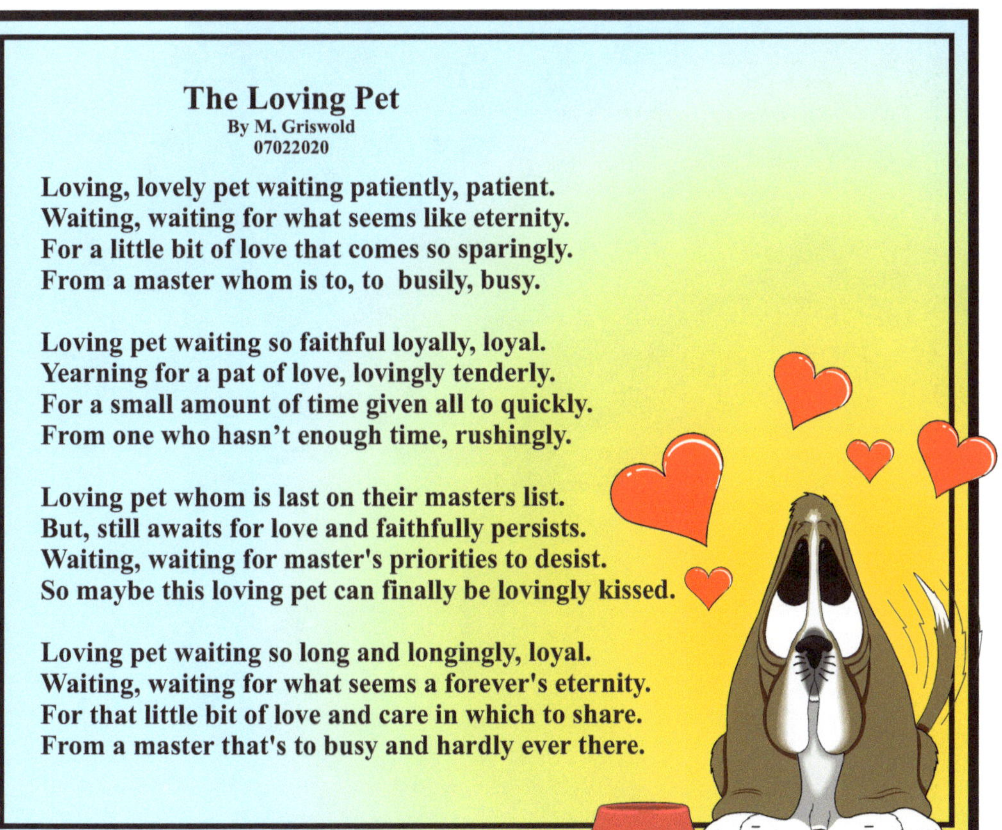

The Loving Pet
By M. Griswold
07022020

Loving, lovely pet waiting patiently, patient.
Waiting, waiting for what seems like eternity.
For a little bit of love that comes so sparingly.
From a master whom is to, to busily, busy.

Loving pet waiting so faithful loyally, loyal.
Yearning for a pat of love, lovingly tenderly.
For a small amount of time given all to quickly.
From one who hasn't enough time, rushingly.

Loving pet whom is last on their masters list.
But, still awaits for love and faithfully persists.
Waiting, waiting for master's priorities to desist.
So maybe this loving pet can finally be lovingly kissed.

Loving pet waiting so long and longingly, loyal.
Waiting, waiting for what seems a forever's eternity.
For that little bit of love and care in which to share.
From a master that's to busy and hardly ever there.

Only If
by M. Griswold
07192020

Only if the timing had been right.
Only if I didn't hold you so tight.
Only if this love was meant for now.
Maybe it would've worked, somehow.

I tried to force destiny too fast is seems.
I tried to realize too quickly our dreams.
I tried to make it all happen just so.
Now, understanding it's late, I must go.

To late the sorrows, to late the tears.
All that's left is an empty love's fears.
With a chest heaving full anger and pain.
I don't want to hurt you, so I can't remain.

I must travel a journey which is deep within.
To make me worthy of your love again.
I must now wait until the timing is truly right.
To love once more and hold you closely tight.

I will return to you after this journey's end.
To pick up those pieces and begin once again.
Only if you will just hold on and wait for me.
Only if the timing is true for our love to be.

Slivered Moon Calling
by M. Griswold
08072020

As I gaze into the sunset's half lit sky.
Spying with my searching naked eye.
The Moon in it's brilliance as a sliver.
Oh, the romance in heart does quiver.

That heavenly splinter shining brightly.
Fills me with joy in love's hope nightly.
Engulfing me with it's rays of hot passion.
Reflecting to thee in true loves bright fashion.

A celestial transference that needs no wires.
This sliver of Moon delivers wanting desires.
With speedy fullness, not losing any portions.
Connecting all of my deep reaching emotions.

In the blackness of void it radiates with force.
Focusing so intently, thus racing it's course.
Limitless in it's measure of love it can carry.
This sliver of moon forces won't every terry.

Then, quicker than a wink, before I can blink.
A feeling of love enters me like slow moving ink.
It is your message of caring and love given to me.
By a slivered Moon's magic in romance's purity.

To Ride a Wild Pony
by M. Griswold
08092020

To ride a wild pony is to know that which is in me.
The good, the bad racing in a struggle to remain free.
How can I endure the bucking and battling combat.
Twisting, turning, tossing it's spirit this way then that.

I didn't expect this when accepting Christ's own creed.
With it's a tremendous force of a charging great steed.
This wild pony has most assuredly turned inside me.
Now trampling and stomping with it's gait's intensity.

I try to restrain this pony's passion and rearing spirit.
All that I can truly hope for is to barely hold on to it.
With tears that now come, streaming out of control.
A pony's seat dripping, small wet pieces of it's soul.

Fearing for it's life as sanity races, raging far away.
I reign in hard this pony's frantic wild ride to stay.
Nothing I do will aid to slow it's frantic mad pace.
Oh God, Please help me, I pray your sweet grace.

To ride a wild pony is a pleasure from within it's pain.
The pleasure is knowing your true spirit with no refrain.
The pain is the agony of facing it honestly raging away.
I ride my wild pony minute by minute of every long day.

To Mend a Broken Heart
by M. Griswold
06222020

To mend a broken heart what medicines do I use.
What salves does one apply for healing to infuse.
Is there needle and thread to stitch it's torn edges.
Or sorrow's tears to wash away the jagged ledges.

Never meaning to shatter the love coming from you.
By the careless words or thoughtless acts that I threw.
I pray it's not to late to heal the damage that I've done.
My heart is sorrowed from the selfishness I have spun.

I cry for your forgiveness of causing you such awful pain.
To retract those hurtful words I said without any refrain.
This spirit kneels lowly, it's core is truly, wholly forlorn.
 I beg redemption for any agonies I selfishly have born.

Therefore, I ask humbly, you forgive this remorseful heart.
And together mend the pieces, bit by bit, every broken part.
Knowing what I ask of you is unfair and me you may reject.
Because of the broken heart you hold and savagely protect.

Someway, somehow, please grant me that grace within you.
To release the pain I've caused and try to begin again anew.
For I yearn for that special someone that's lying deep within.
To let our love's bloom blossom beautiful, forever once again.